LIVVY SKELTON-PRICE

What's Left

What's Left by Livvy Skelton-Price

First published by Livvy Skelton-Price 2025

Second edition
ISBN (paperback): 978-0-473-76928-4

Cover art by Marie Tulbo
Editing by Stacey Clair
Proofreading by Mo Skelton
Beta-Reader: Lutfah Mahmud
Beta-Reader: Eloise Chakour
Beta-Reader: Nicole Dalby

This book was professionally typeset on Reedsy.
Find out more at reedsy.com

This book is dedicated to everyone trying to thrive in a world not made for them.

Chapter 1

Jordi Blount sat on the couch in the permanent dent on the left most cushion. She held a Playstation 5 controller in her pale white hands and focussed her full attention onto the murders she was committing for her online team of a free game she found on her PS5 from the previous owner. Jordi's curly brown hair flopped all over her greasy face which she kept trying to puff away with the force of air from her mouth. Her hair fell in unwashed locks, like ropes hanging down from tree branches. Her pink and yellow banana themed pajamas she was still wearing were soaked in sweat due to her lack of thought to turn on the air conditioning. Jordi's character on the screen fell over in a pool of blood and the words "Killed by sexallday696969" popped up on the screen. Jordi let out a sigh like she was the master of wind and wished to create a gale. She kicked the innocent coffee table sitting in front of her, patiently waiting for a bowl of cereal or a piece of fruit to be placed on top of it but instead the table only received perfectly clean feet and greasy PS5 controllers.

Jordi chose to be the same character - the chick with the biggest boobs, because why not? She went back into play and sent her warrior/fantasy girlfriend into battle. She had her throw a hand grenade and hide behind a wall. Her jaw fiercely chattered like she wanted to eat the breakfast she neglected to make for herself. Another character showed up behind her fantasy girlfriend and punched her until she fell on the ground and a splash of red covered the screen. Jordi bit down on her tongue in frustration and caused blood to ooze into her mouth, she sucked away the iron tasting liquid and picked the same girl again. The game stopped. The words "Your team lost" stood in the middle of the screen, rubbing it in how terrible Jordi was at her favourite game.

"Stupid dumbass team," Jordi cursed, passing the blame.

A quiet yapping filled the room. Jordi looked around to see where the phantom noises were coming from. Her eyes stopped on a fluffy white cloud with four legs, her mind was still fuzzy and focused on the game but Jordi stared at the white cloud, trying to remember where it came from. The little cloud opened its tiny mouth and let out a wolf-like howl, then he or she grabbed a little tennis ball the size of two finger nails put together and dropped it in Jordi's lap.

"Oh shoot." Jordi remembered what this thing was. "Billy T. James, I forgot to take you for a walk!"

Jordi removed herself from the dent in the couch cushion and forced her unused legs to the door which led to the outside world. Jordi threw it open and took a step back, the sunshine hitting her like the grenade her character threw. Jordi swung around to protect her eyes and stared into her dark cave.

"Billy T. James, come on," Jordi tapped her thighs, "come on, doggo, time to go outside."

The cloud look-a-like yipped but stayed in place.
"Come on, little guy," Jordi whined, "just go outside,
please, you'll have fun, I promise."
Jordi picked up the tennis ball the size of two finger
nails and threw it out the door onto the concrete. Billy
T. James just looked at her.
"I think I know what you might like, " Jordi said, "This
is only for special occasions. But I think right now is
the perfect time. Are you ready?"
Billy T. James yipped in reply.
Jordi went into a cupboard and pulled out a cardboard
box with a picture of a waterslide and kids playing and
laughing. She let the box fall to the ground before
yanking out a red, flat, piece of slimy tarpaulin.
"Ew, it's all soapy," Jordi said, flicking it in front of her
to get rid of the sticky creases.
Billy T. James's tail started wagging in circles, he
bounced onto the couch and started yipping and
barking as if he were a full size wolf.
"Woah, calm down, mate," Jordi said.
Billy T. James jumped from the back of the couch onto
the floor, on two hind legs he bounced up and started
biting at the waterslide. He jumped around in a circle,
yipping and barking for all the neighbours to hear.
"I'm sorry," Jordi shouted at the little fluffy ball. She
dropped the waterslide on the ground. Billy T. James
ran at it and slid along the ground with a tail like a
windmill in a hurricane.

The basement stairs started to creak as Jordi's Great-
Aunt, Barbara, came down the stairs. Barbara
carefully placed each foot slowly on the next step and

used the walls surrounding the stairs to balance herself. Barbara was 79 and needed support around the house. She struggled to walk up and down staircases but she braved this difficult venture when she needed to talk to her Great-Niece, Jordan, as projecting her voice caused her more trouble than walking down the stairs. Barbara wobbled on the last step but regained her balance just in time. She grabbed the doorknob at the bottom of the stairs and with all her energy she turned it with both hands and pushed through the door.

Barbara looked at her great-niece who was 22 and capable of so much yet she spent her days sitting on the couch in the basement locking her brain into a world that didn't exist.

Most of the time.

Billy T. James had half his fur slicked back with partially dried soap and wild eyes darting from one end of the room to another. He ran to the start of the slide with his dribbling tongue slapping his furry face. "Jordan, Billy T. James needs to be taken outside," Barbara stopped and looked at the mess that was the basement. She saw a coffee table fallen over, and flicks of soap and dog saliva flying around the room. Billy T. James stopped. He swivelled his head towards the speaker and sprinted to her ankles. The smell of old soap and sweat invaded Barbara's nasal. She brought her hand up to wave away the invisible imposter near her nose, "why are you subjecting Billy T. James to all of this?"

"It's not that bad," Jordi said, "and the door's open."

Barbara held the door to the stairs wide open, "Billy T. James, please free yourself into the upstairs."

The dog sat down with a waggy tail and looked up at Barbara with awe in his eyes,

"Jordan, Billy T. James needs to be taken *outside*. Not rolling around making our home filthy," Barbara walked towards the couch, where Jordi slumped down and picked up her PS5 controller. She sunk into the permanent dent in the couch cushion. Barbara walked around the back of the couch so as not to disturb her great-nieces game, "I think the door at the bottom of the stairs needs to be fixed, it took all of my energy just to open it."

Jordi glanced at where this voice was coming from but the game pulled her attention back instantly.

"I don't know why you like it down here so much," Barbara said, picking up the waterslide and shoving it back into its cardboard box, "Jordan, you must have a shower today. Do you hear me?"

Jordi kept her focus on the screen, "It's my day off," She mumbled.

"Jordan, I had a delightful conversation with my sister just now," Barbara sat down next to Jordi on the couch, pretending the smell no longer bothered her, "she said she has recovered from her cold and as you know colds can hit us pretty hard at our age," Barbara checked Jordan's face to see if she was listening, "I'll just carry on chatting, I know you need to concentrate but you can listen at the same time. I was thinking of going out to bingo tomorrow but my girlfriend had her license taken away because of her eyesight. Honestly, it's about time. She has been seeing double for months, I always grip onto the door handle very tightly when she drives me. Oh, not the door handle, not since the door swung open that one time. Remember? That was very scary, no, I don't hold onto the door any more. I hold onto that thing, it's above the door," Barbara gestured holding onto the handle above the door, "What is it called?" Barbara asked while placing a hand on Jordi's controller.

Jordi felt the mild pressure of her responsibilities' fragile skin as she watched her character die in her game.

Jordi's face went bright red, she slammed the controller onto the couch, sinking it in between the cushions and causing the buttons to dislodge into the abyss that was the darkness underneath the couch cushions. Jordi looked straight ahead towards the screen as she watched her game end, she could feel steam pouring out of her ears as she tried not to scream at the vulnerable figure next to her.

Barbara stood up off the couch, her eyes sparkling with the essence of tears, "Do not treat my things this way," she croaked, "you are not a child," she composed herself, "you are a grown adult and you do not live under this roof for free, I think you should remember that," Barbara walked back towards the door using the back of the couch to balance her, "you need to join me upstairs for a cup of tea, I think," she walked slowly out of the room. Her composure was waning as she turned her back towards her angry and incompetent carer.

Jordi threw herself face first on the couch and started kicking and punching the cushions like a three year old that had been denied a lolly pop at the checkout of a supermarket.

Barbara took one step at a time, slowly and deliberately. Her body shaking from emotion. She had always known Jordi had a temper but lately it had been getting worse and occurred more and more out of no-where. Tears fell out of her tear ducts as she quietly sniveled alone on the stairwell. Billy T. James, the dog, cowardly sulked up to Barbara's ankle and whimpered at her feet.

Jordi was beside herself, her anger was controlling her body and she kicked and screamed without a thought.

After a hot minute Jordi took a breath in.

Her anger seemed to have left her.

She looked around the room at the mess she had made and guilt washed over her like a powerful wave. Jordi stood herself up and went through the door and up the stairs to see if Barbara was okay.

She found her Great-Aunt sitting outside in the courtyard. Barbara was already sipping on a cup of tea and staring out at the overgrown trees on her molding lawn.

"Barbara?" Jordi said tentatively.

"You sit in that seat," Barbara said, pointing to a chair on her right, "And you be a good girl."

Sheepish and embarrassed, Jordi walked over and sat in her assigned seat.

"The lawns need to be mowed. The fountain needs to be de-moulded. The garden chairs need to be replaced. The trees need to be trimmed. And I want laughter to fill this home," Barbara sipped her milky white English Breakfast tea.

"You're being mean," Jordi whispered.

"This needs to be done by tonight."

Jordi's foot started tapping, "It's my day off," she said.

"The children are scared of this house and I don't blame them."

Jordi's mind started buzzing, "It's my day off."

"You ge a day off whe.."

Jordi was no longer listening.

"Jordan!"

Jordi snapped to.

"Stop hitting your hands on your thighs and pay attention," Barbara stood up, "What am I going to do with you?"

"It's my day off. I only work-"

"Everyday seems to be a day off for you," Barbara looked towards the ground and took a long, loud deep breath, "Jordan. When your mum and I decided you would move in to take care of me, we didn't discuss days off. We discussed-"

"What?" Jordi looked at Barbara in disbelief.

"You can have a day off when your chores are done," Barbara said, "my business went under because of you, and I don't want you to forget that."

"It wasn't because of me," Jordi said in disbelief.

"This is your decision," Barbara said, "do as I ask and repay your debts or find somewhere else to live. But be warned. I know everyone who knows everyone in the property business."

"So, you're saying I have no other option?" Jordi asked.

"Exactly," Barbara said, "I need to see a bit of gratitude from you Jordan, and I want you to start referring to me as 'Grandma.'"

Chapter 2

Jordi sank low in her chair as she watched her great-aunt wobble away, each step heavy with the weight of her body. Barbara moved with her hand along the wall as she leaned 2cm to her side. The sun glared into Jordi's eyes which she blinked away like particles of dust. She poured herself a cup of tea from the teapot she had told her great-aunt was vintage china but was actually on clearance sale at T2.

Jordi hated English Breakfast tea. She sipped her putrid drink, feeling the scratch of the unwanted liquid as it reluctantly went down towards her stomach. She scrunched her face just as a bulky woman walked up behind her. A body builder would be anyone's first guess.

"What did you do to Barbara this time?" The woman asked, she towered over Jordi, blocking the burning sunlight from reaching Jordi's pale white skin.

"Nothing," Jordi said, slumped in her chair, feeling the heavy weight of guilt sitting upon her chest. She continued sipping her yuck tea without looking up.

The woman sat herself down in the seat next to Jordi. She picked up a cup that was pink and floral with a gold rim. This woman poured herself a cup of brown, muddy coloured tea.

"Oh," she said, she put down the mug on the small, round mosaic table.

"Yeah," Jordi looked up at her friend, "how's life with you, Faith?"

The woman's short, black hair was slicked back almost as if she'd run a glue stick over it. And if you looked close enough you could see a hint of blue eye liner poking out between the eyelashes. The woman's dark skin went exceptionally well with her dark blue tank top which conveniently showed off the fact that she went to the gym on a regular basis.

"I got myself another gig."

"No way!" Jordi sat up in excitement, "Where?"

"Tell me what you did to Barbara," Faith said in a stern tone. Her eyes pierced Jordi, making her shrink back in her chair.

"I might have blown up at her a little," Jordi said, turning her head away from her friend. The tantrum she threw replayed in her mind and heat burned up her skin as the guilt and embarrassment grew.

"You have to treat her with respect," Faith said, "she's older and more fragile than you."

"I know, I know," Jordi said, wringing her hands together in her lap, "I try."

"Try harder," Faith looked around at the neglected outdoor space, "As much as I love looking at weeds, do you want to do karaoke in the basement?"

A hint of a smile flickered across Jordi's face as they got up from the table. Karaoke was the only game Faith would play on the playstation. They left the mugs and teapot to be cleaned by fairies that only lived in their brains and skipped down the mahogany stairs towards Faith's favourite pastime of belting out karaoke tunes in the privacy of Barbara's home.

They played Tracy Chapman's 'Fast Car' turning their cellphones into microphones.

Jordi sat down in her favourite cushion that made her sink into a V shape. She read the lyrics playing on the TV screen as she sang off key. She fought her mind to not be absorbed into the thoughts of her game from this morning, but the more she fought the stronger the image became. Blood, grenades, running, her team needed the win.

Her mind jumped back to the present moment and she read the words "I'll get promoted."

Her mind flicked back to the conversation with Barbara, she was meant to be cleaning, cooking, caring, working. But Faith was here, and she couldn't disappoint her friend. She felt like there was a rope being pulled in two different directions but all she could do was sit still and try to focus on the- what was she meant to be focussing on?

It felt as though she had no control over the thoughts in her own mind. They skipped, hopped, and jumped without her permission.

Faith threw herself onto the couch and lay flat on her back. She stretched her legs out and used her toes which had been shoved in socks and shoes on a hot summer day to tickle the cheeks of her absent minded friend.

Faith then jumped up and down on the couch shaking her butt and singing at the top of her lungs. She grabbed Jordi's hands and pulled her to bounce on the couch cushions with her. They danced and sang, a smile creeping up on Jordi's face. Jordi decided to jump off the couch flailing her legs, as rockstars do,

and accidentally kicked the coffee table across the
room, along the residue left by the water slide and into
the wall, they heard it crack.

"You okay?" Faith asked as she paused the music and
knelt down to check on her friend.

Jordi stared up with large puppy dog eyes, "I'm okay."

"Maybe we should clean up the soap?" Faith pulled
her friend back up to her feet.

"I-"

The door at the bottom of the stairs swung open and
Barbara stood in the doorway with her hands on her
hips. The women looked at her, stock still in shock.

"Faith, please leave," Barbara said with the sternness
of a burnt out teacher, "Jordan. I don't care if it's your
day off. You need to cook dinner, you need to open
the curtains and you need to clean up after yourself. I
thought I had made this clear."

Jordi just looked at Barbara with a dumbfounded
stare, painfully aware of her friend's presence.

"You need to take a shower, at the very least,"
Barbara added, with obvious exhaustion.

"I agree," Faith said.

Jordi's cheeks burned red and she felt her entire body
burn up in flames.

"You need to leave now, please Faith," Barbara turned
to make room for her to exit up the stairs and away
from the basement.

Faith put her phone back in her pocket and tiptoed
past Barbara with an attempt to make herself tiny
enough to turn invisible. She looked back at Jordi who
shifted her gaze towards the ground and gave her
armpit a subtle sniff. The air around Jordi's nose felt

like a landfill and she blinked furiously to keep the smell at bay.

Barbara and Jordi could hear Faith bounding up each step towards the main entrance.

Barbara gave Jordi a stare which spoke paragraphs. Jordi sulked as she headed towards the bathroom and got herself ready for a shower.

"Once you're clean, you need to begin dinner," Barbara stated as she made her way back up the stairs, Billy T. James wagging his tail and waiting for her at the top stair.

At the dining table, Barbara placed two candles on the long wooden, Soho 2400 rectangular dining table. The lighting was low as the bulbs on the roof had blown months before. The heavy, purple, Luxury Modern Velvet curtains hung, still drawn across the windows covering up the dim, evening sunlight just as they had covered the bright sunny day.

Jordi plated up steamed eggplant and courgette on a side of plant-based chickenless chicken nuggets.

The plates were cold with water residue from the dishwasher that never seemed to be unpacked. She placed the meal in front of Barbara who had already seated herself with a hand sewn napkin laying over her lap.

"I appreciate the steamed vegetables," Barbara said as Jordi sat down opposite her, "But the chicken nuggets are, what I would consider a unique choice."

"They're chickenless."

"What?"

"There's no chicken in them."

With great difficulty, Barbara tried to hide a look of disgust, "What's in them?"

"Soy."

Barbara took a deep breath in, she had never heard of soy-chicken nuggets and she wasn't a big fan of chicken nuggets in general. A small amount of regret rose up in her stomach, 'perhaps,' she thought, 'I should've cooked dinner myself.'

"Jordan," Barbara began, twirling a chickenless chicken nugget on her fork, "Are you prepared to take on more responsibility as we discussed earlier?"

"Yes," Jordi mumbled as she took a bite of eggplant.

"Jordan, I say this because neither of us are quite happy in this situation currently. I can't imagine you're happy living in your tip downstairs, and I'm not very happy about it either. I think you know you are welcome to go back to your parents at any point. Your mum would of course be sorely disappointed at this failure on your part and I would have to demand her share of my sister's inheritance to repay your debts but I'm sure she'd take you back never-the-less. I would like to say, I am very close to sending you back whether you want to go or not. How would you feel about that?"

"Not good. Mum will need that money," Jordi said, "she wants to buy another house in the Coromandel."

"She would never achieve that dream, unfortunately," Barbara said in condescension.

"Oh," Jordi said, suddenly finding it hard to swallow her soy nugget.

"I'll be talking to my sister next week and I would like to report some good news to her. Good news for you of course."

"Whatever." Jordi said in non-compliance.

"I don't understand you," Barbara's eyes shot a look of dominance towards Jordi, "I give you everything, as a Grandmother does, and you give me absolutely nothing in return."

Jordi mumbled away as she ate her chickenless chicken nugget.

"Are you sorry?"

Jordi kept chewing with a full mouth.

"The basement? The couch? Your game? You know you work for those," Barbara's eyes started to fill with tears, "you are supposed to look after me!"

"I'm sorry," Jordi said, sending spit flecks across the table, "I'm trying."

"You need to try harder," Barbara used her napkin to wipe away her tears Jordi was sure she was faking, "As you know my birthday is coming up and the family won't be able to make it over from Waiheke this year."

"Why not?"

Barbara let out an exasperated sigh, "Read the news, Jordan. There's been a problem with the grapes or the grass or something important," Barbara waved around a steamed eggplant on her fork, "now. I would appreciate it if you put in special effort this year. As you know, I'm turning 80 and I always imagined this birthday to be filled with all our family, so I would like you to plan something spectacular for me and my friends, please."

Jordi looked up, "of course."

"One that I will love."

"I will try."

"I wrote my birthday on the calendar in the sitting room so you have a reference if you forget the date," Barbara's eyes fell towards her dinner plate.

"Can you just share it with me?"

"19th February."

"No, I mean-"

"What?"

"Nothing, thank you," Jordi ate another chickenless chicken nugget without any tomato sauce. "Wait, isn't that-"

"What?" Barbara snapped.

"In two days?"

"Yes," Barbara said, "I imagine you've already got most things sorted as we were expecting to have the family over, all you need to do is a bit of adjusting to make it a bit more enjoyable for us older people." Jordi's nerves sent vibrations throughout her body and she began to visibly shake. She was jobless and throwing Barbara a special birthday would require using money. Her government benefit of $360.50 per week barely covered enough for all the coffees, snacks and new games Jordi enjoyed treating herself with. She wasn't sure how she was going to make this stretch to treat Barbara as well. Not to mention she had completely forgotten about Barbara's birthday. She hadn't heard a word from her family. She wrung her hands in her lap. Organisation and planning were not part of Jordi's skill set, she felt her brain beginning to buzz and she tried to focus on her breathing. Barbara was saying something else but Jordi let the words fade into the background as her brain-buzzing got louder and louder.

Chapter 3

Barbara got up from the table and hobbled towards her bedroom without saying goodnight.

Jordi was left with her buzzing brain and the pile of dishes to clean up. Her bones felt heavy after the day of discussions with Barbara and the lack of food.

Seven chickenless chicken nuggets and a spoonful of vegetables weren't enough to store a lot of motivation inside Jordi's tired and unused body.

Throwing the dishes into the dishwasher was a nice distraction from the buzzing and anxiety bouncing through Jordi's head. She slammed the door of the dishwasher closed and pressed start, forgetting to add any soap.

To congratulate herself for a job well done, Jordi went to the walk-in freezer and pulled out a tub of Duck Island Salted Caramel Cacao Crumb Ice Cream and went to her basement apartment to play Selena Gomez's 'Who Says' and give herself a pep talk.

Jordi opened her phone to find there were no messages from anyone. Usually, she didn't mind this. But today she wished she had a text from her mum. She went to type a paragraph but deleted the message. She scrolled through their past conversations which were long paragraphs from Jordi with only a thumbs up emoji in reply.

She fell asleep on the couch with the open ice cream tub on the floor next to her, her head fallen into the couch dent and a fluffy little Billy T. James asleep on her stomach, both of them full of ice cream.

Barbara awoke from her slumber on her Royal Serene mattress and pulled back her Baltic Linen sheets. Waking before sunrise was something Barbara prided herself in. She preferred to have herself ready and presentable for the day before the entire neighbourhood. Her clock read 05:07. The sky was still dark. The stress of looking as though she were the most productive person in the room was strong in Barbara's bones.

Barbara sat up at her dark wood, handcrafted vanity dresser she had inherited from her father. Her silk dressing gown flowed across her back onto her cloud-soft carpet. She analysed her face in the mirror and pushed her cheeks up to remember how she looked 40 years ago. She flattened her skin on her forehead as she remembered how she looked when her skin was young and tight. She didn't have a refuge basement apartment or a gaming addiction back then, but she was new to the big city just like her great-niece.

Barbara looked at a framed photo sitting on her vanity of her parents and eight siblings back when she and her siblings were in their teens and 20s. They were all gathered outside their childhood home on Waiheke Island right before her parents were to drop her off at the ferry terminal to start her journey in the big city. She thought about the way she was going to carve a path for the future generations and make the transition easier for anyone who would follow. She was going to

be the first of her siblings to work and earn a living for herself. Her parents talked about following her but never did. Their stocks grew and grew, as did their vineyard, building more wealth for the family. They stayed back on the Island of Waiheke as the family began to grow and expand; grandchildren were born and the new parents cried out for help and attention. Her parents never even visited her in the city. They were too busy with their grandchildren.
Something Barbara could never provide.

Barbara put on a pair of white, three quarter length pants and a floral blouse that had puffy sleeves the length of her elbow. She loved a good puffy sleeve. Barbara picked up her Philip B Russian Amber Imperial Gold Masque and contemplated whether or not she had the energy to put this through her hair today. She decided she didn't and put on her Louis Vuitton Fedora Black hat instead.
With one last look at her family picture, Barbara threw on her Birkenstocks and headed toward Jordi's sleeping quarters fit for a hard working lass.

Jordi stirred in her uncomfortable sleeping position, waking to puppy kisses from the five year old dog that had spent the night with her on the couch. Barbara stood over Jordi and smiled at this show of affection. "Good morning, Jordan," Barbara said, sitting next to her on the couch. Jordi pushed the dog onto the ground and sat herself up with grunts of disapproval.

Jordi looked at her biological great-aunt and pretend grandmother.

"I'm off to 'bingo and breakfast' with the girls this morning. Could you drop me off please?" Barbara asked.

Jordi looked at Billy T. James whose tail was going round and round like a windmill as he received pats from Barbara.

Jordi nodded her tired head.

After a quick shower, Jordi threw her long hair into a messy bun with a black scrunchie and sprayed herself with Taylor Swift's Wonderstruck Enchanted perfume Barbara had gifted her for her last birthday. She pulled on a pair of light blue barrel legged jeans and a white singlet.

"I'm ready," Jordi said as she exited the bathroom.

"You look lovely," Barbara said.

Jordi stopped, looking taken aback. Compliments were not something she was used to, especially from her great-aunt. She shook it off and followed Barbara out the side door of the basement into the carport.

Barbara handed Jordi the keys. She felt the sharp edges of the metal and tried to guess which car these belonged to. The coolness of the keys was a pleasant sensation in the summer heat, she thought these might be for the Tesla but they could also be the shape of the Mercedes.

"What car are we taking?" Jordi asked, squinting her eyes as the sun bounced off the concrete, burning her retinas.

"The Tesla," Barbara said as she pulled her fedora down past her eyes, "help me, dear."

Jordi put her arm through Barbara's, feeling the light weight of her skin move aside for the heavy weight of her bones. With effort, Jordi guided her as she hobbled towards the gleaming white Tesla Model Y.

"Oh dear," Barbara said as Jordi turned the car on and rolled the windows down, "It's a bit hot."

The heat was hitting the both of them from inside the car like a heavy cloud of fog and a thick puff of steam. The humidity inside the car was suffocating. Jordi didn't worry about her seatbelt, she drove the car out of the driveway to allow some airflow through the car like a hurricane, all the while blasting the air con. Barbara turned her head towards the open window and let the air rush at her.

"Jordi! Jordi!" Barbara yelled, glancing back at her great-niece, "put your seatbelt on!"

Jordi stopped at the end of the driveway to follow her not-quite-grandmother's instructions. Barbara turned her face back the man-made gail force winds through the window.

Jordi pulled up to the Remuera Club where the Bingo games were held. She found a spot right outside the entrance door. Jordi kept the car running as Barbara pulled herself out of the car, using the open car door for support.

"It'll be a couple of hours. I'll give you a ring when I'm done," Barbara said as she closed the car door, "please have the house tidy by the time I need to return home."

"Of course," Jordi said.

"Thank you," Barbara's bottom lip wobbled. Subtle but it was there. Jordi wondered what could be bothering her. A sunny summer day and games with friends, it was more than Jordi felt she had.

In her grandmother's Tesla she sped off away from the towering houses of Remuera. She kept driving until she saw single story homes with large front lawns and families outside teaching their children to ride bikes. Pre-teens stood outside dairies with hokey-pokey ice creams and t-shirts with pictures of pickles on them. Jordi pulled the Tesla to the side of the road and called her friend Michelle.

"What?" Michelle said, answering her phone in a tired whisper.

"Can I come over?"

"Yes," Michelle hung up.

Jordi stood outside her friend's entrance door. She looked at the light brown pine wood that stood at the same height as her. The door frame was as wide as she was and she sucked in her belly to make herself look as small as she could, before she lifted her knuckle to knock.

A short, stout little lady with bouncing gray hair answered the door with a big smile. She wore a long cardigan and sweat pants while her feet were bare. Her toenails shone a bright painted pink.

"Jordi!" She exclaimed, opening her arms wide, ready for an embrace.

"Maggie!" Jordi shuffled sideways and put one arm around this lovely lady, squeezing her arm around the shoulder.

"Come in, come in," Maggie bent down towards the carpeted floor in the hallway and moved some old Banana grocery boxes from Pak'n'save that decorated her walls and floor. These boxes were filled with old kitchen gadgets and broken plastic toys.

"Sorry for the mess," Maggie apologised.

"What are you doing with these?" Jordi asked as she watched Maggie drag one box down the hall.

"Just doing a little clear out," Maggie said, trying to hide the fact she was already puffing.

Jordi shuffled in sideways and continued to shuffle all the way towards the open plan kitchen, living, and dining room. The kitchen island looked out towards glass sliding doors that reached from floor to ceiling and looked out onto Maggie's slightly overgrown garden. She had a vegetable patch with fallen over tomatoes and an overgrown blackberry bush that Jordi remembered falling into once on her first time visiting this house. She had always opted to stay indoors since then.

"Oh Jordi, love," Maggie said, holding onto her sides and puffing openly, "I've been asking around all the businesses near my work but no one seems to be hiring at the moment. I'm so sorry, love," Maggie looked at Jordi with pity in her eyes.

"Thanks, Maggie," Jordi said.

"Have you been looking on SEEK?" Maggie asked.

Jordi shrugged, "yeah, but everyone wants at least two years experience and I have none."

"I'm sure something will pop up," Maggie took a moment for a breath, "It might not be soon but for now you have your Grandmother to take care of which is just so special."

"I guess," Jordi said.

"But you're not here to see me, I'm sure. Michelle's in her room," Maggie pointed to the pale wood door off to the side of the open space living area.

Jordi ambled into Michelle's room without knocking, she closed the door softly behind her and stepped over a pile of clothing to reach the bed where Michelle lay. Michelle wore a large, oversized black top she bought from a concert once and her hair was sticking out in all directions.

"Hey," Jordi said as she climbed into bed next to her friend.

Michelle, a young woman with long, dark brown hair and lightly tanned skin lay in her bed with the covers pulled up to her face. Michelle's blackout curtains were drawn and no light was getting in. Jordi could hear the birds singing outside as the sun was inching towards full height.

"You okay?" Jordi asked, holding her face close to Michelle's, "tired?"

Michelle nodded with her head still on her pillow.

"How long have you been in bed?" Jordi asked in a whisper.

"A while," Michelle mumbled.

"Days?" Jordi blinked away the tears she was hiding. Her friend who used to bounce with joy and chase her down the street on her tricycle was now hauled up in bed, bound by the cuffs no one could see.

Michelle nodded, her eyes closed with heavy weight. Jordi slowly and carefully got out of bed, trying not to disturb her friend. She tiptoed around the room picking up pieces of thrown clothing and placing them into Michelle's washing basket. Her mini skirt lay lifeless on the ground, her sundress sat limp, and her running shoes only peeked from underneath her bed. Michelle didn't stir.

There was a soft knock on the bedroom door and Maggie poked her head in.

"Do you kids want something to- Oh, Jordi, you don't have to do that. Thank you," Maggie's motherly eyes became glossy, "I'll make you something to eat." Maggie sniffled as she closed the bedroom door.

Jordi gathered all the clothes and pulled the curtains wide to let the sun in. Michelle turned under the covers.

"You don't have to get up," Jordi said, "but you need some sunlight."

Michelle pushed herself up into a sitting position.

"Do you feel like getting dressed today?" Jordi asked. Michelle glared at her as she moved her lower body through invisible mud until her feet touched the floor. She pushed herself into a standing position.

Michelle's eyelids looked heavy as she fought them to stay open.

She walked to the door, opened it and left her bedroom. Jordi followed with the now full washing basket. The corners digging into her thigh.

"Michelle, baby," Maggie threw her arms around her daughter in a tight squeeze, "sit down, sit down, I'm baking biscuits. Sit."

Maggie ran out of the room as fast as her bare feet could take her, she came back holding a comb and a box of what looked like spray bottles.

"Jordi, sit," Maggie waved her hand.

Jordi sat down next to Michelle at the kitchen island. Maggie began spraying Michelle's hair with a little white bottle until a cloud of chemicals formed around her head. Maggie then picked up her brush and began yanking at her daughter's knotted hair.

"Ow. Mum. Ow," Michelle said as her head bounced back and forth.

Ding.

Maggie put the brush on the counter and raced to the oven, throwing open the oven door and letting out a soft, sweet smell of freshly baked cookies into the living area. Maggie grabbed a tea towel that was half lying in the sink and half on the bench, threw this over the cookies so a bit of the material hung over the edge of the oven tray and pulled out the cookies with her bare hands. She dropped the tray on the bench in front Michelle and Jordi.

"Be careful, it's hot," She said as she went back to tidying Michelle's hair, "Jordi, Barbara's birthday is coming up soon, isn't it? I was thinking of sending her some flowers," Maggie said as she aggressively pulled apart the birds-nest in Michelle's hair.

"It is, yes."

"Now, what date exactly? I want to make sure I don't miss it."

Michelle's head flopped forward.

"You okay sweetie?"

"Fine," Michelle said, with as much aggression as her mother had been combing her hair with.

"Good, good. So Jordi, when is it?"

"Oh," Jordi said, "I'm not sure off the top of my head. I think it's the day after tomorrow, but she put it on the calendar at home. I can text Michelle the date later."

"Please do, she's so lovely, I would like to do something nice."

Jordi sat and ate the cookies while Maggie yanked at poor Michelle's untidy hair. She had almost completed her task when Jordi's phone vibrated with a text from Barbara to pick her up.

"I had better go. Thanks for the biscuits," Jordi said as she jumped down from the stool and headed out towards the Tesla.

Chapter 4

Jordi pulled into the carport with Barbara next to her. "Thank you for driving me, Jordan," Barbara said, "I have been looking forward to coming home to a clean house, so I appreciate the work I know you put in."
Jordi got out of the car and waited as Barbara hobbled around the bonnet and attached herself to Jordi's arm. They walked to the door that allowed entrance into the basement from the carport.
"Do you have the key?" Barbara asked.
"Which key?"
"The key to the door," Barbara said sternly.
Jordi looked at her with a hint of confusion and turned the doorknob, revealing the door had been left unlocked.
Barbara sighed a heavy sigh, "I guess you weren't gone for that long," She let go of Jordi's arm and walked into the basement.
She stopped.
Jordi walked ahead of her.
She stopped.
The basement was a mess. The TV was no longer on the wall, plaster and wallpaper littered the carpet, couch cushions were thrown everywhere and the pool table was missing.
"Jordan," Barbara said in disbelief.
"How?" Jordi stood as her mouth fell open.

Barbara slowly stepped into the basement.

"Follow me, Jordan," Barbara said, reaching out for Jordi's hand. She had a new found strength about her as she led Jordi into the unknown.

Jordi held Barbara's hand but crouched behind her as they walked.

"Hello," Barbara called, "Hello?"

No answer.

"Jordan, I want you to explain this."

"I...I... Can't," Jordi stammered in disbelief. A wind blew through the open door, Jordi jumped two feet in the air with fright. She heard a creak and squeezed Barbara's hand in an abnormally tight grip. Barbara squeezed back.

"Please," Barbara stated as though this one word was a full sentence. "One of us needs to be calm. I choose you."

"But what happened?" Jordi asked.

"It looks to me," Barbara said with a shake in her voice, "someone left the door open. And the gate. And other people took that as an opportunity."

"No," Jordi shook her head, "No, it wasn't me, no."

"Now is not the time to shrug off blame, Jordan." Barbara said with her voice getting shaky.

"I'm...I'm..."

"I would like to hear you say it."

Jordi looked up at her great-aunt with tears in her eyes. They glistened with fear and anxiety. Her heart pounding out of her chest, even Barbara could hear it.

"Do you have remorse?" Barbara asked, "for being so careless," she too had glistening eyes.

Tears spilt over Jordi's cheeks and she whispered, "I'm scared."

"Jordan, go look upstairs for me, please," Barbara said, letting go of Jordi's hand, "go see what other damage there is."

Jordi looked back at her frail grandmother with a face of stone. Arguing felt as pointless as taking Michelle to the gym. She tiptoed as quietly as she could into the sitting room. Everything looked like it was still in its place. Except for a vase that was broken on the floor and the walls no longer displayed the paintings Jordi loved.

"They just took the paintings," Jordi called.

"Just?" Barbara called back in her faint, elderly voice. Jordi continued tiptoeing around the house but couldn't find anything else that was taken or broken. The foreboding dining table where Barbara enjoyed giving her lectures still sat in the centre of the room under the broken lightbulbs.

The kitchen looked sparkling clean and filled with cold memories of unpaid labour. In the piano room no speck of dust had been shifted. Not until Jordi opened the door to investigate the room, she coughed as she exited, feeling the tickle of particles in her nose. She slammed the door and vowed never to go back in there.

The guest room looked as beautiful as ever. A plushy queen size bed, mini bar and a view of the street the community paid a lot of money to keep clean and polished. Barbara's room was also untouched.

Jordi made her way back to Barbara who stood nervously at the top of the basement stairs.

"They took some artwork from the sitting room but that's all from upstairs," Jordi said as she watched a little fluffy cloud emerge from a slightly ajar cupboard. Billy T. James let out an anxious yet happy whine that sounded like a tire letting out air from an invisible hole.

"Baby," Jordi bent down to give the fluff ball a few scratches.

Barbara walked into the sitting room and lowered herself into her plush armchair, the colour matched Billy T. James's fur.

"Come sit with me," Barbara patted her lap and watched Billy T. James excuse himself from Jordi's affection. He jumped up and curled into a ball on top of Barbara.

"What are we going to do?" Jordi asked, sitting down.

"I'm not sure," Barbara said, "you were only gone for a few moments so I don't know how this would have even happened," Barbara smiled as Billy T. James licked her nose.

Jordi shuffled her feet nervously. She knew quite well she had irked her responsibilities and visited her friend instead. Barbara had asked her to clean up the house and instead, she had left the house unlocked and unattended for hours.

"Yeah," Jordi said.

"It only takes a few minutes to get to the club from here. Considering you took a lot longer than expected to pick me up, I imagine you were busy cleaning, and then you would've only popped out for five minutes. Tops. You obviously didn't lock the door when you left but surely you would've locked the gate. It doesn't seem realistic that all of this could have been done in five minutes."

Jordi watched her great-aunt play with her dog. She knew exactly what Barbara was getting at and the guilt burned a hole in the pit of her stomach.

"Billy T. James is such a happy boy," Barbara said, "I mean, you would have had to leave both the door and the gate open for someone to come in, and you probably had to be elsewhere for the entire time I was at bingo-and-breakfast otherwise I don't think this could've occurred."

Jordi said nothing.

"They must have been watching the house. Trucks and movers would've been used. It would've been quite the operation."

Jordi could feel herself wanting to combust. The pain in her stomach grew and spread throughout her body. Barbara scratched behind Billy T. James's ear as he tilted his head to look up at her.

"It's just so sad all of your hard work has been wasted. I think I'm going to have to have a lie down."

"But what are we going to do?" Jordi's words burst out.

"I think you need to think about an answer to that, yourself," Barbara said as she pushed Billy T. James off her lap and stood up.

"But... But..." Jordi stammered. "Grandma."

Barbara ignored Jordi and continued walking towards her bedroom.

Jordi's phone buzzed. It was a text from an unknown number. "Don't forget to tell me Barbara's birthday. Hope you got home safe xoxo - Maggie.

Chapter 5

Jordi walked back down the stairs, she sat on the very last Mahogany step before the door into her empty basement and brought out her iPhone 16 with 256GB. Jordi dialed "111"

"Hello. Police, Fire, or Ambulance."

"Police," said Jordi.

"Address."

Jordi gave her great-aunts address.

"Nature of the crime?" The person on the other end of the phone asked.

"Our house has been robbed," Jordi said.

"Are you currently safe?"

"Yes."

"Is there anyone in your house who shouldn't be?"

"No."

"Please hang up and either dial 105 or fill in an online form on police.govt.nz to report crimes which are a non-emergency."

The phone line went dead.

Jordi stared at her phone in disbelief. She shook her head as she typed police.govt.nz. She followed one link to another link to another link to another link. She made it to the form which said "please allow 15 minutes to complete this form." Jordi clicked "Get

Started." And then put her head back onto one of the steps.

She contemplated whether or not filling in a form for 15 minutes was worth her time and if it would even lead to any fortunate outcome.

But then she remembered her free online game and if her great-aunt bought her a new PS5, it wouldn't have her saved progress.

Jordi sat up and began filling in the form.

After an hour and a half, she completed the form and put her phone away in her pocket.

"Grandma!" Jordi called as she made her way up the stairs. Jordi made her way into the sitting room. The walls looked bare without the paintings.

Jordi made her way over to where the calendar used to hang. A bright white rectangle patch was the replacement. 'What a strange thing to take.' She thought.

"I suppose it's how they knew we were out," Jordi said out loud. She looked to where her favourite painting used to hang, a lighthouse in front of a moody sky and angry ocean, she used to love wondering what caused the elements to have so many emotions.

"Jordan?" Barbara said sleepily, as she came into the sitting room. She had changed into her Karen Walker Love Letters Silk Wrap Pj Set for her nap.

"I filled in a form for the police," Jordi said, "I gave them your number."

"Very good," Barbara said, "I look forward to their phone call."

"What do we do now?"

"You're a big girl, Jordan," Barbara said, "I need more sleep, this has been quite traumatic for me. Can you figure this out on your own?"

Jordi looked at Barbara's stern face.

"Yes."

"Thank you," Barbara turned around and made her way back to her bedroom, "Thank god I have my party to look forward to," Barbara said in a casual, didn't even realise she was saying it, non chalant kind of way.

Jordi's jaw almost dislocated from how far it dropped. Once her mouth was ready to close again, she called Michelle.

The phone rang from the bench that was still holding the last biscuit from the freshly baked batch of chocolate chip cookies Michelle's mother had smothered her and Jordi with.

Michelle had migrated over to the couch with a view of blue skies and chaos outside her glass doors.

"Your phone's ringing!" Maggie called from the bathroom.

Michelle didn't answer. She watched as her stomach moved up and down with every breath that she took.

"Your phone!" Maggie called, walking into the room and picking it up herself. "It's Jordi!"

Maggie clicked the green answer button on the screen and held the phone to her ear.

"Hello, Jordi, this is Maggie," Maggie listened, "What!? Jordi, I'm so sorry. You did? Okay, that's good. No, that's all you can do. You did the right thing..."

Michelle let her Mother's piercing voice bounce over her as she closed her eyes and focussed on the feeling of her lungs expanding and her ribs moving every time she allowed oxygen to enter into her body. "Michelle, honey," Maggie called as she ran into a different room, "Jordi needs us," Maggie ran over to the washing basket Jordi had placed in her living room. Maggie gave it a quick scan and pulled out some dark blue flare jeans.

"These will be fine," Maggie placed them over top of Michelle's tired body, "put them on."

Michelle felt the heavy weight of the denim fall over her and she felt the button cut into her stomach.

"It hurts," Michelle said.

A puff of chemicals flew into her direction and all the oxygen she was enjoying disappeared in an instant. "No time to shower," Maggie said, "oh, that smells delightful. You got me that when you were a child." Michelle sat up and watched the jeans fall off her and onto the ground. She stared at them as she thought about the effort she needed to exert to lift them up, lift up each foot, push her weight through the heavy material, pull them around her waist and then button them up with her fingers which already felt like they were overworked carrying her skin. These thoughts flooded Michelle's body with exhaustion and her bones felt like 50kg weights holding her in place.

"Come on," Maggie said. She bent down and began dressing her daughter. Maggie slipped jandals onto her child's feet, "no getting out of this one, I'm afraid. You can sleep in the car."

Maggie allowed her daughter to lean on her as they walked towards the car. She buckled Michelle into the front seat as she stared forward, very little life glinted in that poor girl's eyes.

"I'll buy you some Burgerfuel," Maggie said as she pulled out of the driveway.

"Okay," Michelle said in a small voice.

"And a thickshake?"

Michelle nodded. She adjusted her small, underweight body in the front seat of her mums black Subaru Impreza.

The seatbelt pressed into Michelle's bones and she could feel the edges slicing into her skin with how suffocatingly tight this belt was holding her to her seat. She hated how she felt, her energy seemed to leave her body with every breath she took. She couldn't explain the cause or how to fix this. All she knew was that she was tired and every inch of her body hurt.

"I got you and Jordi chocolate soy-thickshakes, one V8 vegan and three bio-fuel burgers with kumara fries," Maggie handed Michelle the food and drinks. Michelle held the ice cold thickshakes in her hands and felt the stabbing of each water drop on the cups, like needles shooting through her skin. The heat from the warm food on her lap melted through her jeans and onto her legs like an iron melting plastic. Michelle stayed like that, simultaneously freezing and burning until her mum pulled into the driveway on Arney Road.

"I'll take those, you take the food," Maggie said, grabbing the thickshakes from her sullen daughter, "oh, they're a bit cold."

Maggie took the drinks and rushed inside, not bothering to wait for her daughter. She threw the door open and let out a scream, throwing her hands up but keeping a tight grip on the thickshakes.

"Michelle, come look," Maggie called.

Michelle lifted one leg and guided it to the ground. The second leg reluctantly followed. She sat and watched as her mum held the door to the basement open so she could have a view of the tragedy.

Michelle looked across with a blank face. She could see the gray carpet was speckled with white from the walls and the pool table which could normally be spotted from the driveway, was missing.

Maggie ran inside, out of sight.

Michelle lifted an arm up to the top of the car door. She paused to regain a steady breath.

Her mum miraculously appeared next to her, wrapping Michelle's arm around her shoulders and lifting her to her feet. She guided Michelle into the house and up the stairs, all while keeping an eye on the food and holding a hand underneath it in case Michelle's grip gave out.

Maggie placed her daughter gently on Barbara's Luxury Classic Sofa "Maestro" in black. She took out the kumara fries and a BioFuel burger and placed these next to Michelle. Jordi reached over and handed a soy-thickshake to Michelle who drank it like it was life support.

"Thank you," Michelle said after finishing the entire cup.

"Feeling okay?" Jordi asked.

Michelle shrugged and ate a kumara fry.

"I brought food for everyone," Maggie announced, "we can put Barbara's in the kitchen, the poor thing. This would have rocked her completely. Thank god you were here, Jordi."

Jordi grabbed the bag of food and took out her V8 Vegan, she inhaled the burger and then sat back in her seat sipping on her thick shake.

"I also told Faith what happened."

"Good," said Maggie, triumphantly, "you need all the support you can have right now. Did you call your family?"

Jordi nodded, "I left mum a message."

"Good," Maggie stated, "And for now, Barbara needs to know you're here for her."

"I just wish they'd come over and help me."

"They have their vineyard, dear," Maggie said, placing a hand on Jordi's shoulder, "If that stops, everything stops. Running something like that isn't for the weak."

Jordi sighed as she opened Tik Tok on her phone and began scrolling.

"Jordi," Michelle said in her tired tone as she lifted her arms up signaling to her friend she wanted a hug.

Jordi moved from the armchair to sit next to Michelle on the couch. Michelle wrapped her loving arms around her best friend, "are you okay?"

"Not really," Jordi said, wrapping her arms back around Michelle.

"I came as soon as I heard!" Faith burst into the sitting room.

"Faith!" Jordi stood up and squeezed Faith in a tight hug.

"What's been happening?" Faith said to a stone faced and droopy eyed Michelle, "you doing okay?"

Michelle gave a weak shrug.

"Look at you!" Faith said, letting go of Jordi and putting her fingers around Michelle's wrist. "You're so thin!"

"She had BurgerFuel just before," Maggie piped up, "and I know she needs to eat more." Maggie started to walk over to Michelle like a Mother Hen protecting her flock from the opinions of the outside world.

"Oh, no, it's okay," Faith said, placing Michelle's arm in her lap, "I just know she's been sick but I think you're looking after her so well."

"Oh," Maggie said, looking sheepish, "thank you. Actually, I had better go and check on Barbara. The poor woman must not know what to do with herself."

"Sorry Michelle," Faith said, "how are you doing?"

"Fine," Michelle shrugged, "It's not about me."

"What is there to do, Jordi? You've contacted the police, right? So what do we do now?" Faith asked.

"Sit and wait, I guess."

"That can't be right," Faith shook her head, "If you don't hear from the Police, you need to follow up."

"What's the point?" Jordi whined, slumped in her chair, "they already did the crime."

"Jordi," Faith looked at her with a stern face, "when a criminal takes something from you once, they are likely to come back and do it again."

"Thanks. Seriously. I wasn't worried enough," Jordi sank lower into the chair, giving no impression she was in the least bit worried.

"This is serious, Jordi."

"Is it?" Jordi said as the tip of her head reached the corner of the couch, "I gave them Barbara's number so she can handle it."

Faith looked at Jordi with disappointment.

"You can stay at mine, Jordi," Michelle said. She stopped to take a few breaths, "you and Barbara can both stay."

"Thank you, Michelle."

"Where's Billy T. James?" Faith asked, suddenly in a panic.

"With Barbara," Jordi mumbled.

"That's fine then," Faith's face went from anger to concern.

Maggie creaked open the door to the sitting room and peeked her head in.

"Oh, Jordi," Maggie said, "I think you had best go check on Barbara. She isn't doing well."

Faith jumped up from her chair, "I'll do it, Maggie."

"No," Maggie said sternly, "I asked Jordi. She needs her granddaughter, off you go."

Jordi sat up from her chair, kept a tight grip around her phone and headed towards Barbara's room.

Chapter 6

"Jordan, is that you?" Barbara asked from her Royal Serene mattress and her Baltic Linen sheets.

"I'm here," Jordi said.

"Good, darling," Barbara croaked in a voice that sounded like she had overused it at a concert the night before, "Come here."

Jordi knelt next to her great-aunt's bed and took her hand with her soft fragile skin and curvy-from-arthritis fingers.

"This has been quite a traumatic event for me, as I'm sure you know," Barbara looked solemnly at her great-niece, "a woman at my age should not be going through such things as this."

She patted Jordi's hands.

"And I know it wasn't your fault, dear. You were being a good girl, you were here doing your very best, I know that. I can see you've been trying."

Barbara turned her head away from Jordi.

"This is so hard for me to say," Barbara croaked.

Jordi squeezed her great-aunt's hand.

"Oh, Jordan. I don't think I can tell you. You are so
precious. I know none of this was your fault."
Jordi didn't say anything. She held her great-aunt's
hand and watched her struggle to get the words out.
Barbara gave a weak little cough.
"Are you okay?" Jordi asked. Her eyes glistened with
tears, "Grandma?"
"Nothing you need to worry about, my dear," Barbara
took her hands back and slipped them under the
covers. She closed her eyes and let her head fall
slightly to the right.
"I'll let you rest," Jordi whispered as she slowly got up
to her feet.
"Jordan?"
"Yes?"
"Can you get me a glass of water?" Barbara's voice
was barely audible.
"Of course," Jordi gazed down at her great-aunt. She
had always seen this woman as someone who was
harsh and demanding. She had never taken a
moment to see her for her fragile self. She looked
down at the pale white skin which never saw any sun.
Jordi was always too busy to go on walks with her
when the sun was out. The thinning hair on her head
was in desperate need of a salon visit, a place Jordi
was always too busy to take her to and too forgetful to
book. Jordi watched as Barbara's mouth parted, so
gentle. The air going in and out through her lips made
Jordi wonder how many more times Barbara's body
would be capable of allowing that. She had so many
stories from her real grandparents about Barbara's

head strong ways and her fighting attitude to get through almost anything.

Jordi couldn't imagine that now.

Jordi turned and waded her feet through the plush carpet that was as white as the day Barbara had installed it. The soft fluff that Jordi felt was as soft as candy-floss and as white as the clouds on a sunny day.

"Jordan?" Barbara croaked.

"Yes?" Jordi turned towards her frail great-aunt.

"I need ice."

"Of course," Jordi said as she went to the kitchen.

Jordi came back with a glass of water and one ice cube in a Cristina Re Rose Crystal Tumbler. She held it out to her great-aunt who attempted to sit up on her elbows but fell straight back onto her designer mattress.

"Jordan, I can't," Barbara said, "I'll need a tray."

"That's okay," Jordi looked around the room and moved her hand which was holding the glass towards Barbara's dark wood vanity.

"No, Jordan," Barbara said, at an almost normal volume, "take the glass with you, there is nowhere to put it here. Bring it back on a tray."

"Of course," Jordi turned around and walked out of the bedroom holding the glass of water.

She went back to the kitchen, found a wooden serving tray, put the glass in the middle of the tray and carried it back to her great-aunt.

"Here you go," Jordi said, holding the tray out.

"No, no, no," Barbara said from a fully seated position with her back against the headboard. "Look at this. Does this look nice to you?"

Jordi looked taken aback.

"No. I'm sorry, Jordan, but I need it to look nice. With all the stress, I need a little bit of beauty to help me take my mind off things," Barbara raised a hand up to the corner of her forehead with her palm faced out. She stared off into thin air.

Jordi looked over at the wall facing her great-aunt's bed. There was a beautiful painting by Pierre-Joseph Buc'hoz of a soft pink Hyacinth.

Jordi looked back at her great-aunt, turned around and did as she was told. She returned with a hand embroidered napkin folded into a square, placed in the corner of the tray.

"No, Jordan," Barbara said, upon Jordi's return, "go find me a flower and a vase. That's the least you could do."

Jordi looked over at the painting again and looked back at her great-aunt. Barbara had turned her head to the side and closed her eyes once again.

"Sorry, grandma," Jordi said. She took herself and the tray back to the kitchen. She placed the tray on the stainless steel bench and looked around at the industrial sized kitchen fit for a team of caterers.

Jordi poured out the water into the sink and re-filled it with a bottle of Fiji water, she then placed three ice cubes carefully to make only a little splash. Jordi went into the walk-in fridge and found a bunch of roses their local florist had placed there for Jordi to display whenever she would get around to it. They looked a

little wilted and the petals were heavy with water but
Jordi thought this was good enough. She pulled the
petals off and sprinkled them on the tray around the
water glass. She took the embroidered napkin and
threw it over her forearm. She also cut up an apple,
squeezed lemon juice on the pieces and sprinkled
pecan brittle over the top. She placed this in a crystal
bowl she bought for her great-aunt from Bed, Bath
And Beyond but told her it was from a vintage auction.
Jordi placed this on the tray and took it to her great-
aunt.

"Thank you, Jordan," Barbara said as Jordi placed the
tray on her knees and laid the embroidered napkin
over her lap.
"I hope it helps you feel better," Jordi said as Barbara
took a sip of water.
"Oh dear, Jordan," Barbara said.
"What's wrong?"
"This tastes like it's from the tap. Please take it back
and pour me the water we have in the fridge. We have
endless bottles of Fiji water. Please, Jordan," Barbara
shook her head.
Jordi's mouth fell open.
Jordi took the tray back. She walked into the kitchen.
She immediately turned around, walked back into
Barbara's bedroom and gave everything back to her
great-aunt.
Barbara took a sip from the glass.
"Thank you, Jordan," Barbara said. "That's much
better."
Jordi's mouth fell open again.

"This is the way you should be taking care of your grandmother," Barbara said in approval.

"Yes," Jordi agreed, "maybe I should call her."

Barbara turned her head and glared at Jordi.

"Well," Barbara said with a sharp tone, "be sure to inform her about what has happened to me."

"Yes," Jordi said, "and to me too."

"You may go now, Jordan," Barbara said, "but make sure you come back to check on me, as you are aware I am very weak."

Jordi gave her great-aunt a glance before walking out of the room. There was something about her pale, soft skin. She didn't look as weak as she claimed she felt. The way she crunched on her apple was loud and hearty. She was sitting up on her own and her tone no longer had the hint of death. But then again, shock can do crazy things to people, she was best not to over think it.

"Goodbye Jordan," Barbara said, stern.

"How's Barbara?" Maggie asked when Jordi came back into the sitting room.

Jordi let out a heavy sigh and slouched down in one of the armchairs.

"She has food and water," Jordi said in a wobbly voice.

"Oh Jordi," Maggie said, wrapping her arms around the young girl, "you've both been through something so traumatic."

Jordi snivelled but didn't say anything.

"I think you are going through a bit of shock. You'll be okay, I think you both are a bit distressed and you both need rest," Maggie gave Jordi a little squeeze, "she'll be okay. Oh, you poor thing."

"Mum?" Michelle said with a weak voice, "can Jordi come stay with us?"

"Oh, no Mimi, my baby," Maggie cooed, "Jordi needs to stay here, I don't think Barbara is in a state that will make it easy for her to move. She needs her own bed and all the comforts of her own home."

"But who will take care of me?" Jordi snivelled, "I don't have any of my own things."

"Oh now," Maggie said a little wearily. She looked over at her daughter with the heavy bags under her eyes and the t-shirt she had worn for the past three days, "why doesn't Michelle stay here with you?"

Michelle looked at her mum with tired and desperate eyes.

"It'll be good for you Mimi, you can have a different enviroment and that might liven you up." Maggie said, patting the cushions, "Jordi, I'm sure you'll appreciate the company. You two can have sleep overs in the lounge like when you were young."

Jordi nodded, "In a different house under different circumstances though."

"It makes me so happy to see you out and about," Maggie tilted her head and her eyes sparkled as she admired her daughter.

Michelle looked over at Jordi who looked back with pleading eyes.

Michelle looked back at her mum, "I can stay."

"Stay here and get some rest," Maggie stood up from the couch, slapping her knees right before she did so. Maggie turned back towards her daughter, "I honestly think you'll feel better being out and about and away from your dirty room. I'm going to clean it and then I can come back and collect you. I'm sure you'll feel better soon."

Michelle's eyes filled with tears of exhaustion.

"It's okay, Michelle," Faith said, "you can lie down." Michelle lay herself down, feeling the soft thread of the cushions. She could feel her heart rate slow and her breathing even out as she lowered her head closer and closer to the couch cushion. The tears that threatened to become overflowing liquid slowed in its tracks as Michelle closed her eyes. She could hear her friends mumbling in the background but she couldn't focus on any one thing, or on what any one person was saying. She knew she was there to help Jordi and knew her friend needed her. She knew this wasn't about her and she didn't want to be a big lump of annoyance sleeping while her friend was anxious, worried and scared. She didn't want to be a burden. But her bones felt like they were made of stone, her breath was heavy as it passed through her lungs and she couldn't open her eyes. She tried. She tri-

"Jordi, I can stay with you too," Faith said.

"Thanks," Jordi said, "she's asking for so much."

"That's besides the point," Faith said, not even blinking before answering, "of course she's asking for a lot. You need to take care of her and you need to look after Michelle too."

"But who will look after me?"

"Stop saying nonsense," Faith said, "I'm here to look after you."

Faith stopped. She looked over at Michelle who had fallen asleep even before her head had hit the cushion.

"What do we think is wrong with her?" Faith asked.

"No one knows," Jordi said. She looked at her friend with pity, "she's had so many fluctuations in her energy like this for months. She might just need a few more days of rest before she can get up and walk around again."

"It's been like this since she had Covid, right?"

Jordi nodded, "we do know that she needs sleep and that is what she is getting. So don't wake her up."

"Do you think it's worth Michelle seeing a doctor again?" Faith asked.

"She's seen so many of them but they're all useless," Jordi said, "she's been to so many doctors, so many times. No one can find a cure, or a diagnosis, it's up to her to find out what works now. And what works is rest."

"You sleep on that couch," Faith pointed, "you need rest too."

"Alright," Jordi said, laying herself down on the couch opposite Michelle, "we can top and tail if you want?"

"Jordi, have you locked the doors?" Faith asked.

Jordi shook her head, "no."

"Go and do that then," Faith said, waving Jordi off.

"No way," Jordi said, reeling back, "I'm not going downstairs."

"Oh my god," Faith looked at Jordi with annoyance, "you're an adult."

"It's scary," Jordi whined, "I don't know who came in or what they were wanting and I never want to go back down there again," Jordi's eyes filled like a bath tub, she turned her face into the cushions to not let her friend see her tears.

"Fine," Faith sighed, "I'll go and lock it then."

"By yourself?" Jordi asked between sniffles.

"Yes, if you're going to be a baby about it," Faith headed towards the stairs that led down to the basement.

"Wait, I'll go with you," Jordi stood up and ran to be at her best friend's side, "no one's going down there alone."

"Are you crying?" Faith asked, looking into Jordi's teary face.

"No," Jordi spat back in self defence.

"It's going to be okay," Faith said, squeezing Jordi's hand, "we're doing this together."

Faith took Jordi by the arm and squeezed her tight as they creaked open the door that led down to the basement.

"What if someone's hiding down there?" Jordi asked.

"The worst decisions lead to the best stories," Faith said, "and you love a good story."

"I do," Jordi nodded.

They both took in a deep, shaky breath as they took their first step. The creaks along the stairs were loud and rang in Jordi's ears. They both wobbled on the third step which seemed to have some bounce in the mahogany wood. Still linked, Faith and Jordi reached their spare hands out and used the wall to guide them as they descended the staircase.

The door at the bottom of the stairs loomed towards them. Closed. Blocking off the memories and trauma that lay beyond.

"Are you ready?" Faith asked.

"No," Jordi said, "but I'll never be."

Faith lent forward, grabbing the door knob. She pushed the door with an extra hard shove and it whined on rusty hinges as it opened.

The two women felt the emptiness of the room before they digested their surroundings.

Wallpaper still littered the floor, the hole where the tv was ripped away sat like a gaping hole in Jordi's sense of security. Her body started to shake. Her feet felt glued to the floor and her whole body went as stiff as a board.

"Stay here," Faith said, unlinking their arms and moving herself forward through the empty basement which was once Jordi's safe space.

Jordi watched as Faith glided across the room, she tried to focus and notice any hazards Faith might be missing but her eyes blurred and her vision turned to static. She heard a ringing in her ears and her brain suddenly felt like a merry-go-round. Her clothes felt itchy and she twitched with built up anxiety.

"All done, we can get out of here now," Faith took Jordi's hand and held it until they were slumped on the couch together back in the safety of the sitting room.

A little bell could be heard in the distance.

Chapter 7

"Did you ring me?" Jordi asked Barbara, entering her bedroom.

"I did," Barbara was sitting up in her bed with her back against a lining of pillows.

"What do you need?" Jordi asked.

"Jordi, we will need dinner tonight," Barbara stated, "and I honestly just need something comforting."

"Of course," Jordi agreed, "do you want me to order us something?"

"Oh no, Jordan," Barbara said, reaching out a hand and grabbing her gently around the wrist, "Let's have a home cooked meal tonight."

"Who's going to cook it?" Jordi asked.

"You, my dear," Barbara said, "I thought of something that is particularly comforting and I know you'll just love making it."

"Is it easy?" Jordi asked.

"It's so easy," Barbara said, "oh Jordi, I had a friend who used to make this for me anytime I fell sick and it's all I'm craving right now."

"What is it?"

"A souffle and brisket. Oh, Jordi, you'll love it,"
Barbara said, "I ate this all the time in my thirties and
it'll really help with the shock of things."
"A brisket?" Jordi asked, "but I don't eat meat."
"You don't have to eat it if you're going to be picky,"
Barbara said, letting go of Jordi's wrist.
"Can we just order something?" Jordi asked, "we're
both going through this."
"Oh Jordi," Barbara brought her hands up to her eyes
and wiped away something Jordi couldn't see, "this
could be my- no. Oh Jordi. No, you don't need to hear
about my problems."
"You can tell me," Jordi said, sitting on the bed next to
her not-grandmother.
"Oh no, it's okay. I just- You never know- I- I just want
to-tonight to be special, that's all," Barbara said as she
wiped what looked like nothing from her dry face.
Jordi bent down and kissed her great-aunt.
"Please tell me what's wrong," Jordi said.
"Oh Jordan. I don't think the world wants me here
anymore," Barbara took her time saying that sentence,
"now go make us a delicious dinner."
"Of course," Jordi nodded, "a souffle and a brisket."
"A twice-baked Roquefort souffle with poached
quince."
"A what?"
"A twice-baked Roquefort souffle with poached
quince," Barbara repeated, "and a black braised
brisket."
"Oh. O-okay-y," Jordi stammered.
"Please Jordan," Barbara begged, "for me."

Barbara placed her hand on her heart and looked up towards the ceiling.

"I do, really care for you, Jordan," Barbara said, while looking up towards the heavens.

Jordi nodded and left her great-aunt's bedroom.

"Is she okay?" Faith asked as soon as Jordi walked back into the sitting room.

"She wants a souffle and brisket for dinner," Jordi stated.

"What?" Faith exclaimed in surprise.

"We have to give it to her," Jordi stated, with a hint of desperation, "she needs it."

"Of course," Faith cooed, "we will."

"What the hell even is souffle?" Jordi asked.

"Come on, Jordi," Faith said, "you have to know what a souffle is."

"Why should I know what a souffle is?" Jordi complained.

"It's okay," Faith tried to be comforting, "we'll find out what souffle is."

"A twice baked souffle," Jordi stated, "It's all she wants."

"We could potentially ask Michelle?" Faith suggested, "when she wakes up."

"I mean, she was a chef back when she was well," Jordi said, "she'll know what it is."

"Let's try to google it first," Faith suggested.

"I guess," Jordi shrugged.

She paused and took a breath.

"Do you think something like this could kill her?" Jordi asked.

"What?" Faith sat next to Jordi on the couch and put her hand on her knee, "no, Michelle's going to be fine."

"I mean Barbara," Jordi said, "she seems kind of weak. I feel like she wants this as a goodbye meal."

"Oh Jordi," Faith cooed, "this would certainly put her into shock but I'm sure it won't kill her."

"Hey, Michelle," Jordi said, lightly tapping Michelle's shoulder, "Michelle."

"Don't," Faith said, hitting Jordi's hand away from Michelle, "I'm not sure if it would kill her. We just have to take extra good care of her for the moment."

Michelle didn't stir.

"What am I going to do?" Jordi whined, "all I can make is steamed vegetables and nuggets."

"You'll be fine," Faith said in a matter of fact tone.

"I think this might be killing her," Jordi said, "I think I might be killing her. I should've cleaned the house, I should've looked after the garden."

Jordi threw her head into her hands.

"Yes. You should've done all of those things. But that's not why she's upstairs in bed. She wants a decent meal, that's a good sign. Breathe," Faith tried to be comforting.

"Have you eaten the food I make?" Jordi asked, "It's terrible."

"I'm sure it's not that bad."

"We can just find a place to buy the food and pretend I made it," Jordi said, "Barbara won't know the difference."

"Won't she?" Faith asked.

"I can't find anything on google," Jordi whined, looking down at her phone, "only recipes."

Jordi threw her head back against the cushions.

"I can't do this," Jordi said.

"Yes, you can," Faith informed her, "I'll help you. We'll turn that kitchen into Hell's Kitchen and make the best damn food Barbara has ever tasted."

"Thanks, Fi," Jordi said.

"Now find a recipe so we can go get the ingredients," Faith demanded.

"I can't," Jordi said, holding out her phone, "this is all too much."

"It's not too much," Faith said, "one step at a time."

Michelle started to move on the couch and her eyes slowly fluttered open.

"Morning, sleepy head," Jordi said.

"I had a dream I was a chef again, making souffle and I burnt the brisket," Michelle said sleepily.

"Yes!" Jordi jumped to her feet, "you got this, Michelle. You are the best!"

"Calm down," Michelle said, "you're making me tired."

Chapter 8

Michelle stood in the stainless steel kitchen with a navy blue and white stripy apron. She leaned on the cold bench for support as her friends surrounded her.

"I found a recipe," Jordi said, "a twice baked cheddar souffle. Looks good."

Michelle shook her head.

"Twice-baked souffle with Gruyere and Cheddar?" Jordi asked, "what's Gruyere?"

"A cheese," Michelle said, sucking air into her exhausted lungs, "what cheese does she want, Jordi?"

"I'm not sure," Jordi said from the bench stool she was swinging on, "I don't remember, it was souffle and brisket."

"Can you go and ask her?" Michelle asked, with an irritable edge to her tone, "If we're going to do this we're going to do it right."

"No, please," Jordi begged, "can't we just make her a souffle."

"No," Michelle puffed with little energy.

"Go, Jordi," Faith commanded.

Jordi stomped towards her great-aunt's room.

Michelle sat down on Jordi's stood, "I'm excited. I haven't cooked in months."
"You sure you're up for this?" Faith asked.
"I might need to instruct you guys instead of me cooking," Michelle explained.
"Of course," Faith said.
"Can I still wear the apron?"
"Of course," Faith said again, "you seem way better than you were before. You were a zombie earlier."
"I know," Michelle said, "this disease is weird."

Jordi knocked a quiet knock on Barbara's door.
"Come in," came a croak from inside the room.
Jordi opened the door that boasted a Rosewood finish.
"Hey, Barbara," Jordi whispered.
"Grandmother, call me grandmother," Barbara breathed in loudly.
"Grandmother, what was the souffle cheese you wanted?" Jordi asked.
"Oh, Jordan," Barbara said, "you are so thoughtful to ask. I would like twice-baked Roquefort soufflé with poached quince."
"Okay," Jordi said, sounding dissatisfied.
"Twice-baked Roquefort soufflé with poached quince," Barbara repeated, "and a black braised brisket."

Jordi made it back to the kitchen and repeated what Barbara said. And then repeated it again as she typed it into google.
"I found it," Jordi said, "It's from a restaurant in Melbourne. It's not even a recipe"

"It says it's from Bistro Gitan," Faith read aloud, looking over her shoulder.

"She said her friend used to make it for her," Jordi said in confusion.

"Maybe she knew the chef," Michelle offered.

"Maybe," Faith agreed, "can we cook this?"

"Do we have ingredients?" Jordi asked.

"This is your house, Jordi," Faith said, "you should know."

"How do you make it?" Jordi asked, "what do you need, Michelle?"

"No," Faith said, "Michelle's not cooking, she's just going to instruct us and oversee."

"I thought you were feeling better?" Jordi asked.

"I am," Michelle said, "but not like, better-better."

"Alright, what are the ingredients?" Faith asked.

"We need milk, an onion, a bay leaf, cloves-" Michelle said.

"Wait, slow down," Jordi said, "I'll check that we have those."

Jordi opened the walk-in fridge.

"Faith, hold it open."

Faith walked over and held the door open.

"Milk," Michelle called.

"Yup," Jordi called back.

"Onion."

"Uh, yeah, I think so."

"Cloves?"

"We have a whole cupboard for spices so I'm sure we do."

"Jordi, just go check." Faith said.

Jordi walked over to the cupboard twice the height of herself, she pulled the cupboard out like a sideways drawer. There were four shelves stacked to the top with all different kinds of spices.

"Who needs this many spices?" Michelle asked.

"I don't know, I think it was for the chefs at parties or something," Jordi tried to explain.

"A chef's dream," Michelle said to herself, "can you see cloves?"

"I see cinnamon."

"They're different," Faith said.

"Yeah, I see them," Jordi said.

"Nutmeg," Michelle said.

"Yeah, I see it," Jordi said, looking through all the spice jars at eye level.

"Plain flour."

"Yeah. We have that," Jordi said.

"Rogue-fort."

"What is that?" Jordi asked.

Michelle leaned over the bench to project her voice, "Roquefort, it's a type of blue cheese."

"Ew," Jordi said with disgust.

"It's for your grandma, Jordi, remember that," Faith said, "Chevre?"

"It's a type of goat's cheese," Michelle explained.

"This sounds horrible," Jordi said, "I can't believe Barbara wants this as comfort food."

"Do you have eggs?" Michelle asked.

"No, I think we'll have to pick that up with the cheese."

"We also need cream, caster sugar, a cinnamon quill, star anise and a quince," Michelle read out, "your grandma sure wants a good meal tonight."

"What even are those ingredients?" Jordi asked.

"Use a cinnamon stick instead of a quill," Michelle said, "and a lemon instead of quince. We'll never find one of those at this hour."

"We have those," Jordi said, "we just need the cheese and eggs."

"I'll order delivery," Faith said.

"Wait," Jordi called, "can you also order a brisket?"

"Yup," Faith said, making the order on her phone.

"Alright. Michelle., Jordi said, "what can we do to start?"

Michelle sat at the bench with her chef apron on instructing Jordi and Faith around the kitchen. She repeated instructions and pointed out where items were when Jordi and Faith failed to see what was right in front of them.

Faith's phone dinged. She ran out of the kitchen and returned with a bag full of groceries.

"No one touches the brisket," Michelle said, hopping off her stool.

Faith and Jordi watched and kept a cautious eye on Michelle as she chopped, rubbed, and cooked up the brisket - all while Faith and Jordi fumbled with the souffle.

"I'll go set up the lounge," Faith said, "Michelle, go slow."

"I feel great," Michelle said, "I almost feel alive again."

Michelle plated up the brisket carefully on four plates. She slid a piece of brisket on to the handmade ceramic dinner plate as the room began to spin and her chest grew tight. She paused, leaning over the meat.

"Are you okay?" Jordi asked, running to her side.
"Fine," Michelle said as she picked up her knife to
continue cutting and serving, "Put the. Souffle. Here."
"Sit down," Jordi said.
Michelle took a seat at the bench and watched as
Jordi sliced the meat like she was hacking down a tree
in the middle of the woods. Jordi plated up the pile of
melted cheese they had worked so hard to make into
a Souffle. Michelle tried to smile as she also tried to
breathe through the stabbing pain of jealousy in her
chest.

"Dinner is served," Jordi said proudly to Barbara who
sat expectantly in the dining room. She had hobbled
in, leaning heavily on the furniture as she tried to do
her bit and support the effort Jordi had gone to for her.
Michelle was sitting already, her skin had gone from
ghostly white to a light tan back to pale. She smiled
even though she could feel every muscle in her
cheeks and they felt like they were pulling down on
her skin. Faith sat down at the table, wearing ripped
jeans and a plain white t-shirt covered in flour.
"I had no idea you were both here," Barbara said as
she placed her napkin over her lap.
Faith had placed a runner down the table and laid out
some wilting roses along the runner with lit candles in
between each flower. The lights were still in need of
replacing and the room looked dim.
Barbara smiled, "I see the brisket," She said, "This is
quite impressive. I thank whoever made this."
"Michelle made the brisket," Jordi said, "Faith and I
tried to make the souffle."

Jordi looked sheepish as she took a spoonful of the ruined cheesy mess.

"The brisket is so good," Faith said.

Michelle smiled and took a spoonful of cheese.

"It's nice and soft with a lot of flavour," Barbara said, "the cheese is a bit too strong though."

"It's the blue cheese you like," Jordi said.

"Oh," Barbara looked disappointed, "yes. Good."

Faith told stories about their adventure in the kitchen and boasted about Michelle cooking the brisket.

"Everyone in the country must be missing her as a chef," Faith said, taking another mouthful of brisket.

"You were a chef? Where did you used to work, Michelle?" Barbara asked.

"Wildfire. Down on the waterfront. They do a lot of meat there," Michelle explained, "It was really busy and vibrant, I loved working there but it was stressful."

"And what do you do now?" Barbara asked before taking another bite of the brisket.

Michelle's cheeks burned red, "I'm not working now."

"Why not?" Barbara asked, "what is it with your generation and not wanting to work? Faith, do you work?"

"I do," Faith started, "I work in-"

"Your generation doesn't know what hard work is," Barbara sighed, wiping her mouth with her napkin.

"I do work," Faith said in her own defence, "I go to the office everyday."

"Yes, well," Barbara said, "I suppose that's good."

"I work in administration for a sales company-"

"At least it's a job," Barbara stated.

Michelle pushed herself away from the table, "If you don't mind, I think I'll excuse myself."

"Of course, Michelle, that's fine," Faith said, turning her attention away from Barbara.

Michelle took her plate and left the dining room.

"I always found her a little funny," Barbara commented.

"She's sick," Jordi said.

"What does she have?" Barbara asked, "I don't want to catch it, you know how colds can affect people my age."

"She has Long Covid," Faith explained.

"Long covid?" Barbara asked, "oh I'm sure that's just something your generation made up as an excuse to stay in bed all day. She looks healthy enough."

Jordi's face turned red with anger and Faith looked at Barbara in complete shock.

"Well," Faith began to explain, "she still has some leftover form of the virus, or maybe they're saying it's MS now, or chronic fatigue, I'm not sure. Either way, her energy fluctuates quite drastically and she gets sick often, she's not supposed to exert much energy; overwise she comes down with flu-like symptoms, it's really hard for her actually."

"I don't believe in any of that," Barbara said, "you just need to push through and keep working otherwise there will be nothing left for the next generations. It's about having the right diet and right amount of exercise. I worked through every flu that I had. Your generation is just afraid of hard work, it's embarrassing."

The silence at the table was loud.

"Maybe we should finish dinner now," Faith said, walking the plates into the kitchen.

"Jordi, please take me back to bed," Barbara said, "I'm old, I'm allowed to lay in bed all day." She gave a weak little cough.

Jordi gave Barbara support as she went back to her room, while Faith joined Michelle in the living room. She found sheets in a cupboard and started turning the two couches into beds.

Billy T. James ran into the sitting room and flew into Faith's leg. She crumpled to the floor giggling as the pile of fur climbed on top of her. He turned his tongue onto hypo speed mode and spread his germs all over Faith's face.

"Hi, my baby," Faith cooed.

Michelle lay on the couch, fast asleep with her unusually pale face. She was no longer in her jeans and black shirt, instead she had changed into cotton shorts and a purple plaid button up shirt, left undone showing off a bright white shirt underneath. A damp towel lay near her, thrown over the back of the couch. Her feet were flung on top of the damp towel so she was almost laying upside down.

"We shouldn't have let her help with dinner," Faith said, looking into the pale face she once knew to hold a permanent smile and was blessed with a tan Jordi often expressed jealousy of.

"Sorry Michelle," Jordi whispered.

Chapter 9

"The door is locked, right?" Jordi asked as she settled onto the couch Faith had made up for them both. She pulled the sheet up around her neck.

"It's locked. We locked it," Faith reassured, "we just have to stay calm and be aware of any noises we hear."

"Do you think Barbara will be okay?" Jordi asked.

"Jordi," Faith said, "you heard what she said today."

Jordi sighed, "If I don't take care of her the way she wants me to, she's sending me packing."

"Maybe that would be for the best?" Faith suggested, "find a place that doesn't have such terrible views on the world."

"I'd have to go back to my mum, and Barbara doesn't actually have anyone else in this world," Jordi said, "It's kind of sad."

"That might be for a reason," Faith said, "why don't you at least get a job? Something part-time. That way you can still care for Barbara while standing on your own two feet."

"There's nothing," Jordi said, laying her head back, "no one's hiring, everyone's becoming redundant.

There's no point. And I need to look after Barbara, that takes time."

"I'm sure you'd find the time to do both," Faith said.

"There's still nothing going," Jordi replied.

Faith looked at her poor, lazy friend, "there will be something. Now, let's try and get some sleep." Faith lay her head down on one end of the couch.

Jordi didn't sleep that night. Her brain wouldn't quieten down, thoughts raced around and around. Who broke into the house? Who left no trace? Why would someone do that? Why couldn't Faith keep her feet to herself?

The morning sun rose and heated the sitting room to 29.7 degrees celsius. Faith and Jordi awoke by kicking each other in their wakeful sleep. Michelle stirred and moved her arm through an invisible puddle of quicksand to lay her arm above the blanket.

"Her cheeks are so red," Faith said as she rolled off the couch and folded the blankets up and placed them on the armrest of the over-priced, overly fancy designer couch.

"I had better check on Barbara," Jordi said, yawning. She was still wearing the same outfit she had on the day before. She bounced on her tiptoes out of the room, up the stairs and lightly knocked on Barbara's bedroom door.

"Just a moment," Barbara called.

Jordi stayed outside the room and waited. Barbara had never called for a moment before, it was unusual for her to reject any sort of attention from Jordi, it was more common for her to beg for it.

"Is everything okay?" Jordi called knocking on the door again.

"Come in," a weak, croaky voice called back.

Jordi pushed the door open and walked into the bedroom. Barbara was laying in bed with a full face of make-up on. Her lips were red and her cheeks were a powdery pale. Jordi definitely noticed some sparkle on the eyelids as she looked down to make sure her great-aunt was still breathing at a steady pace.

"Oh, Jordi," Barbara said in a voice that was barely audible, "thank goodness it's you."

"Are you alright?" Jordi asked.

"As alright as one can be under the circumstances," Barbara said, "the police called me yesterday. I told them you've done so well and have everything under control."

"Faith locked the door downstairs so no one can come in now," Jordi said.

Barbara knitted her eyebrows together, "well. Good. I'm glad one of you is doing something."

"We're all doing something," Jordi said, "are the police coming to inspect the place?"

"Jordan," Barbara said thoughtfully, "they will follow up again but I can't guarantee they'll bring back what you lost. Now, I just wish I was up to my birthday party," Barbara shook her head.

"What?"

"You've been taking such good care of me since the incident and I feel awful that I won't be able to enjoy the party," Barbara took a pause.

"We thought you might just want to relax and enjoy time to yourself," Jordi said carefully.

"I'm sure you put in the effort I deserve," Barbara said,
"I'm sorry I ever doubted you."

"It's okay," Jordi said.

"You know what," Barbara said, "carry on with your
plans, I'm sure I'll be up for it, even if it's just for a little
bit."

"Oh," Jordi said, "great."

"You are such a good girl," Barbara patted Jordi's arm,
"now I must sleep if I'm going to get my energy back.
Oh, shock is nasty."

Barbara closed her eyes.

Jordi looked down at her great-aunt who she swore
was wearing a full face of make-up, tucked up under
her Baltic Linen Sheets.

Jordi walked back into the sitting room.

"It's Barbara's birthday," Jordi announced.

"Happy birthday, Barbara," Faith said, combing her
hair back.

"No," Jordi replied.

"Oh," Faith said without emotion, "sad birthday then."

"Faith!" She turned to look at Jordi, even Michelle
stirred on the couch.

"She wanted me to throw her a big birthday party and
if I don't throw her a party, she wants to kick me out,"
Jordi said in a panic.

Faith put her brush down, "I'm sure she'll understand
under the circumstances if you haven't planned
anything."

"She won't," Jordi said.

"It's understandable you forgot," Faith said, "yesterday
was quite traumatic."

"No," Jordi whined.

"Well, *have* you planned anything?" Faith asked, "just go with what you got."

"I've got nothing," Jordi said, "I forgot all about it. But now she's upstairs with a full face of make-up on, resting up so she has energy for the party."

Jordi sat on the couch and put her head in her hands, "what am I going to do?"

"What about your family?" Faith asked, "what have they planned?"

"Nothing," Jordi said, "they're staying on Waiheke. They can't come over, which is why Barbara wants a big celebration."

"Why?" Faith asked.

"I don't know," Jordi whined, "she wanted the family here. But they can't come because of grape reasons. So now she wants to do something with her friends."

"That's lovely," Faith said.

"What day is it?" Jordi asked.

"Sunday," Faith answered.

"Do you think bingo will be on today?" Jordi asked.

"I have no idea, Jordi," Faith said, sternly, "that sounds like something you would know."

"We have to go," Jordi said.

"Where?" Faith asked.

"To The Club," Jordi panicked, "we might be able to find her friends and see if they want to come here for a party."

"Why don't you just take her to Waiheke?" Faith asked.

"She's too old to handle the boat," Jordi said, "and she gets sea-sick."

"Oh, dear," Faith said, "shower first, we all need a shower."

There was a knock at the door, "Police," a stranger called.

Jordi froze.

"I'll get it," Faith opened the front door, "you're here for the robbery?"

"We are," Two women in police uniform stood at the door. They both had flowing blonde hair and red lipstick on.

"Please, come in," Faith gestured for the two of them to enter the sitting room, "the robbery took place downstairs in the basement."

"We'll have a look," one said, "Is it okay if we don't have anyone going down there while we're looking?".

"That's fine," Faith said, "Jordi and I are about to head out. Michelle will probably stay asleep, and Barbara's upstairs if you need her. She discovered the scene with Jordi."

"Perfect, we'll need to talk to her in a bit."

"She's just lying bed recovering from the shock of it all," Jordi explained, "she's in her seventies."

"That's no worries," one of the Police women said, "we'll have a look around first and talk to her afterwards."

Jordi showed them the door to the basement and they took themselves downstairs.

"Let's go," Jordi said as Faith put away her towel and dirty clothing into her backpack. Faith had on a floral sun dress, while Jordi was in jean shorts and a baggy top with her hair tied up in a messy bun.

"Where are we going and how are we getting there?"
Faith asked.

"The Remuera Club," Jordi shook some keys in her
hand, "we're taking the Tesla, baby."

"She gave you the keys?"

"I never gave them back."

"Oh Jordi," Faith said with pity.

"Come on, live a little."

Faith looked at Michelle who was still fast asleep on
the couch, "she'll be fine, right?"

"She'll be fine," Jordi affirmed.

Faith and Jordi walked out the door and through the
overgrown grass that was up to their thighs. They
passed a moulding bird bath with a crack through the
stand, grass grew all over it like a straight jacket.
Fallen branches from broken blossom trees littered
the ground. Vines grew across the wooden gate, the
only thing that held the wood pieces together. Jordi
pulled the twine and winding branches apart, making a
hole for Faith and herself to walk through.

"You get shotgun," Jordi said, shaking the keys in her
hand.

"Of course I get shotgun," Faith said.

"No fun."

Jordi unlocked the Tesla and sat in the driver's seat.

"How? Where?" Faith looked around the car and
under the car, she started tapping on the door with the
palm of her hands.

"What are you doing?" Jordi asked.

"How do you open the door?"

Jordi opened the door from the inside, "It's a secret
only Tesla owners know."

"Very funny," Faith said as she sat down and pulled the door closed. She fastened her seatbelt and looked over at Jordi, "Not too fast in this thing."

"Never," Jordi said with a cheeky smile. She did a U-turn in the driveway and drove out of the gates she had continuously forgotten to close.

"Jordi," Faith warned, "be sensible, please."

"It's a Tesla, chill."

Faith took a few breaths and watched as Jordi stopped at a red light.

"Good job," Faith smiled, "you're actually following the rules for once."

"Always," Jordi gave Faith a glance and smiled.

"How fast can this thing go?" Faith asked, "and what does that screen do?"

"No one knows," Jordi said, her smile growing bigger, "and lots."

Jordi tapped the screen to show the reverse camera. The light turned green and Jordi pressed her foot against the accelerator.

"Don't," Faith gripped the edges of her passenger seat and pressed the back of her head against the headrest.

"I'm going fifty."

"Jordi."

"Alright, fifty one."

"Jordi."

"Okay, okay, sorry," Jordi slowed down to fourty eight kilometres an hour, two kms below the speed limit. Jordi turned onto a tree and car lined street, she parked outside a sign that read "The Remuera Club."

"Let's go," Jordi said, unbuckling her belt and throwing the door open, "be quick."

"How?" Faith asked, slapping the inside of the door.

Jordi opened the door from the outside.

"How did you do that?" Faith asked, stepping out of the car. Faith watched as the door shut but still saw no sign of a door handle.

"A secret," Jordi winked.

Jordi and Faith walked down the driveway and entered into the club that resembled a school hall.

"Can I help you?" A woman dressed in denim shorts and a white t-shirt asked.

"Um. Well. We're-" Jordi stammered.

Faith looked at her, embarrassed and annoyed.

"Do you know Barbara?" Jordi asked.

"Which Barbara?" The lady asked.

Jordi thought for a moment, "Barbara Blount?"

The lady thought for a second, "don't know any Barbara Blounts here."

"She comes to bingo often," Jordi said.

"Look around, mate," The lady said, "bingo ain't on, Barbara's not here."

Jordi looked around at an empty hall that had been coloured a dull orange. Folded tables and stacked chairs lined the walls leaving an empty hall big enough for a game of indoor bowls.

"I want to know who her friends are, she's my great-aunt and I wanted to invite her friends over for a cup of tea."

"Sorry, girl," The woman said, "I know a few Barbara's but not a Blount."

"Her last name might not be Blount."

"Sorry," The woman shrugged and walked away.

"There's no one here, Jordi," Faith said, stating the obvious.

"We need to find her friends," Jordi said, "what do old people like to do?"

"Don't be so rude. They're just people," Faith said, "her friends are probably home on a Sunday morning, do you know where any of them live?"

"No," Jordi said.

"Useless," Faith said, looking around.

"I really thought they'd all be here playing bingo."

"Look, a notice board," Faith pointed to a corkboard hanging on the faded orange wall. The corkboard had paper flyers pinned to every centimeter of the cork. Faith scanned each piece of paper.

"They have indoor bowls this afternoon," Faith said, "does she play bowls?"

"I don't think so," Jordi said, "but that's a great idea."

"Maybe some of her friends will go to that? Jordi?" Faith looked around but could no longer see Jordi standing next to her.

"Excuse me," Faith heard the familiar voice from a far away corner of the room, "do you have to book for bowls?" Jordi asked another woman in denim shorts and a white shirt who was picking up a broom.

"No, you can just show up but if you're not a member, there is an entrance fee," the woman explained.

"Thanks," Jordi skipped back over to Faith, "did you hear that?"

"Yeah," Faith said, "you want to come back and pay an entrance fee to find Barbara's friends?"

"No," Jordi said, her face falling, "we can pretend we're throwing her a bowls themed birthday."
"But where would we get everything?" Faith asked, "from The Warehouse? And who will we invite?"
Jordi threw her hands in the air, "you don't get it."
"No," Faith stated, "I don't get it."
"We bring Barbara here and tell her the bowls *is* the birthday party," Jordi smiled a proud grin.
"Oh, Jordi," Faith said with pity.

Chapter 10

Faith and Jordi pulled up to the house and parked in the driveway.

"Here's the game plan," Jordi said, "we tell Barbara we planned her a party at the club but we only go if she's feeling up to it. If not, no worries."

"Jordi, this is going to be a disaster."

"No, it won't," Jordi said, "just listen."

Faith sighed and looked at her friend.

"I'm thinking we invite the neighbours. She's always talking about how she wants the house to look like theirs and be as cool as theirs and whatever, so I'm thinking she must like them."

"Jordi-"

"No, shh," Jordi said, "we tell them about bowls, they're rich enough they won't care about the entrance fee and maybe we tell them about Barbara being extremely unwell so they come-"

"Jordi!" Faith screeched, "that's unethical."

"No, no, listen," Jordi said, caught up in her own world, "we tell them this and they come. They fill the hall with so many people Barbara won't notice who is there and who isn't."

"I don't know, Jordi," Faith said, "this plan could backfire so easily."

"No, I don't think it will," Jordi stepped out of the car and kept chattering away to Faith.

"If the hall is full and Barbara is not feeling well, she can sit in the corner and relax. We can keep bringing her food and drinks so she doesn't notice no-one is talking to her."

Jordi didn't hear Faith's answer, "what?"

She looked around but couldn't see anyone next to her. Jordi looked back to the car and saw Faith sitting in the passenger seat with her arms folded, looking very cross.

Jordi walked back over to the car to let her friend out.

"Sorry," Jordi said.

"Never leave me in the car again," Faith said, sounding like a dog who just found out their 'walkies' was a trip to the vet.

"Sorry," Jordi said, "so what do you think?"

"Of what?" Faith said, sounding particularly annoyed.

"Of what I just told you," Jordi said, sounding exasperated.

"When?" Faith asked, "when you were out here talking to yourself while I almost died of heat stroke?"

"Oh," Jordi looked down, "sorry, Faith."

They walked back through the unmaintained jungle and back into the sitting room where they found no-one.

"Where'd she go?" Jordi asked.

"You're back," one of the Police women said as they walked into the sitting room, "we've just spoken to Barbara and explained everything but we'd like to confirm a few details with you."

"Sure," Jordi said.

"Did you see or hear anyone when you arrived home?"

"No."

"Did you see or hear about any suspicious behaviour leading up to this event?"

"No."

"And the items that were taken were a couch, a bed, a bedside table, a dresser, pool table, coffee table, tv, and a PS5?"

"Yes."

"Unlucky," one Police woman said as she took notes, "you left the gates and door open, is this correct?"

"The door was unlocked but not open," Jordi said while her cheeks turned the colour of a cherry.

"That would explain why there were no signs of forced entry," she put her notebook away, "look, there's not a lot we can do. We've taken photos and a few samples. We'll run them through forensics and let you know if they show anything. If you do notice any suspicious behaviour, just give the 105 number a call. And lock your doors."

"Thank you," Jordi said.

"Have a nice day," The Police left smiling while Jordi's stomach dropped to what felt like below the ground. Her world suddenly felt empty. Helpless. Jordi suddenly felt like a child lost in the isles of a supermarket.

"Where's Michelle?" Jordi asked, trying to bring herself back to the present moment.

"Let's find out."

Jordi followed Faith into the empty kitchen, then she followed her into the empty dining room, then back to the sitting room and out onto the deck where they found Michelle sitting up drinking tea.

"A tea party?" Jordi asked.

"Barbara brought me some tea, and I thought the sun might help," Michelle smiled her weak smile.

"Barbara?" Jordi asked.

"She came down to see if we needed anything," Michelle leaned her head against the side of the house.

"Did she ask you for anything?" Faith asked.

"No," Michelle shook her head, "she just made tea."

Jordi sat down on the deck, away from the sun and leant back on her arms looking up at her friends.

"Nothing like a sunny day," Faith said, seating herself in the chair next to Michelle's.

Michelle could feel the cold metal against her thighs and the edge of the chair dug into her bones but she was too tired to get up and move. Her cup of tea sat losing heat next to her on the table.

"Are you okay, Michelle?" Jordi asked, "do you want to go back inside and hide from the sun?"

"But the sun will help, she does need fresh air," Faith said, "I can get some ice for the tea."

Faith went inside, grabbed ice and another tea pot full of tea.

"Here you go," Faith said, adding ice to Michelle's mug.

"Thank you," Michelle said with a drained smile.

"We should get you some sunscreen," Faith said.,"Jordi, where's your sunscreen?"

"I don't have any," Jordi said.

"You don't have any?" Faith looked up and down at Jordi's milky white skin, "you're literally glow-in-the-dark."

"I usually just hide from the sun," Jordi shrugged, "I don't really like it."

Faith's face fell open, "you don't like the sun?"

"Why would I, inside, it's so good," Jordi said.

"Help her inside," Faith demanded.

"She might just tan," Jordi suggested.

"I like the sun," Michelle added in her weak voice.

"We can't risk it," Faith said, placing her arm under Michelle's and helping her to stand up.

"Stop," Michelle said. A single tear dropped down along her cheek as she was lifted by Faith's strength.

"I think your cheeks are a little red," Jordi commented, placing her arm around Michelle to help support her as she walked.

"Not helping, Jordi."

"Have you never heard of asking before touching someone?" Michelle said as the tears reached the corners of her lips, "It's called consent."

"Michelle, are you okay?" Faith asked, "you're really quiet."

"She's crying," Jordi noticed.

"Jordi, go get the aloe vera," Faith demanded.

"What aloe vera?" Jordi asked.

"You will be the death of me, Jordi," Faith groaned, they lowered Michelle onto the couch in the living room, "go find some. I'm sure there's plenty in the jungle out there or go to a mystical place called a shop and bring some home."

"That's a lot of work," Jordi said, "I'm sure she'll be okay."

Faith gave Jordi a glare that made her feel like she was about to be evaporated in a bucket of water.

"You can be so sweet and then such a selfish prick," Faith groaned, "I'll go get the aloe vera."

Faith sidled past the furniture in a huff, she tripped over the corner of the couch and nearly flung herself into the wall which donned designer, custom made wallpaper.

"Your purse," Jordi called, picking up a dark blue shoulder bag big enough for a thin wallet and a slim phone.

"Chuck it," Faith said, holding out her hands ready to catch.

Jordi used her rugby arm to throw the purse across the room. She hadn't played a game in years but she still believed she had the same amount of strength. The bag landed on the couch. They both looked at it. Jordi walked towards it as Faith snatched it. She turned on her heel and finished storming out of the room.

Jordi lay back on the couch, "I feel like there was something I was supposed to do today."

Michelle looked over at her friend who seemed so relaxed, just staring up at the ceiling.

"What do you want to do today?" Jordi asked Michelle.

"Dude," Michelle whispered.

"What?" Jordi turned her head and looked at her friend, "yes, I know we're looking after you, but I mean what else?"

Michelle just stared at her.

"What?"

Michelle closed her eyes and let the weight of the world envelope her. The walk from the deck to the couch was not something her body had been ready for. She let herself fall horizontal, the weight of her skin and the weight of having so little control over her life flattened her like gum on the bottom of a shoe. Jordi sat bolt upright, "I don't have a present for her- I don't have a party planned- I don't have anything-" She could feel her breath becoming short and sharp. She tried to suck in the oxygen around her but each breath felt like she was sucking in icicles through a straw. Her chest felt like someone had tied a rope around her lungs and was pulling tighter, and tighter, and tighter. Her world became smaller, and smaller, and darker.

Michelle could hear the panic attack start. She'd been there for many of those, she knew how it went down. Jordi needed a distraction. She needed someone to snap her out of this. She needed someone whose arms didn't ache, eyelids were light, someone who could move across the room to her.

"Michelle?" Jordi heaved.

Jordi kept hyperventilating but she moved next to the head of her friend.

"Hold it," Michelle whispered with all the energy she had left, "I'm right here."

Jordi held her breath, she looked to her friend and longed for her to wake up. She longed for Michelle to spring out of bed. She longed to be held by her.

"I'll count. Just hold it," Michelle whispered. She mouthed the numbers. Jordi watched and nodded. When Michelle mouthed 'six' Jordi let out a slow, steady stream of air. She looked down at her hands and turned them over slowly.

"I'm okay, now," Jordi said, laying her head gently on top of Michelle's.

"Are you okay, Michelle?" Jordi asked.

Michelle said nothing, she lay still with her eyes closed.

"One thing at a time," Jordi said to herself, "I just have to make a plan."

Jordi knocked on her great-aunts door.

"Who is it?" Came a grumpy voice from inside the room.

"It's Jordi."

Jordi could hear a few weak coughs and a very weak, "come in, dear."

Jordi pushed open the door, "are you okay, do you need anything?"

"Oh, my dear," Barbara said from her bed. She had the fluffy Billy T. James laying next to her in the sun.

"Do you have everything?" Jordi asked.

"All I need is your bright smile," Barbara said, looking into Jordi's eyes like a grandma would minus the intense amount of love.

Jordi tried to give Barbara a smile but it came out more as a grimace.

"I'm doing okay, sweetheart," Barbara said, "are you alright?"

"I'm okay," Jordi said, "Michelle isn't too good though."

"No," Barbara said, looking down, "she wouldn't be. I am sorry for what I said last night, she just looked so healthy then."

"It's okay," Jordi said, looking down.

"You are taking such good care of her, and of your dear old grandma," Barbara sighed.

"I like taking care of people," Jordi shrugged.

"Oh, well, good," Barbara said, knitting her eyebrows together, "I would really like to try and go for a walk today, Jordi. Do you think you could clear a path in the garden for my wobbly legs?"

"Bowls!" Jordi almost shouted.

"What?" Barbara said, moving her head away from her grand-niece.

"Bowls," Jordi repeated in a normal volume, "we organised a birthday party for you today at bowls."

"Oh, how nice," Barbara said without any enthusiasm.

"We organised it all and all of your friends are coming," Jordi said, her voice rising higher and higher.

"How wonderful," Barbara said with happiness, "could you clear the path outside?"

"Of course," Jordi said, "but you can reach the car from the basement."

"I never want to go into that basement again, Jordi," Barbara said, "please use your brain."

"Sorry," Jordi said.

"Oh, I hope it's all cleaned up downstairs," Barbara said, sounding weary, "I would hate for those reminders to still be there."

Barbara closed her eyes and sunk back in her bed.

"It's okay," Jordi said, "don't stress. Just hold your breath and it'll be clean by the time you want to re-enter that space."

Barbara gave Jordi a confused look, "okay, Jordan." She waved a tired hand to signal to Jordi that it was time for her to go.

Chapter 11

"I have the aloe vera gel and sunscreen," Faith said, throwing the items on the couch next to Jordi.
"Barbara wants the outside to be cleared, simply because it's her birthday and she wants to be able to walk outside without tripping over," Jordi whined.
"Don't we all," Faith said as she rubbed sunscreen on her arms, "what's the problem?"
"She wants that all done by tonight."
"And?"
"And what?" Jordi asked, "isn't that enough? Isn't that too much?"
"She's been asking you to do that for months now. I reckon you should get to it, here have some sunscreen."

Faith and Jordi walked out the front door and into the overgrown garden.
"I guess we just move everything to the side to make a path?" Faith asked.
"That's not good enough, Faith," Jordi said, "Barbara will want a nice, flat concreted path with little flowers growing all along it and big blossom trees as eye candy. Oh, it's all too much."

"Breathe," Faith demanded, "that's too much pressure, Jordi. Calm yourself"

"But there's no point in having a path if it's going to be messy," Jordi complained, "I'm going inside."

Faith grabbed Jordi by the shoulders and looked into her eyes, "remember why you're doing this."

"For Barbara. For my mother. For me."

"We don't need to be designers," Faith said, "just make it walkable."

"Yeah, alright," Jordi grumbled.

"We can make it as beautiful as you want but the first step is to move the branches out of the way," Faith said.

"Fine," Jordi bent down and picked up a fallen branch from a once beautifully blooming blossom tree. She threw it to the side like a toddler throwing a tantrum.

"Great," Faith said with faked enthusiasm. "I love it when you're in this mood."

"So I just do that?" Jordi asked, "and make this part clean and the rest messy?"

"I couldn't care less if I'm honest with you, Jords," Faith said, looking around at the garden.

Faith helped Jordi throw branches into the abyss that used to be a garden fit for a magazine. They stopped at the gate falling apart with twine barely holding pieces of wood together.

"Now what?" Jordi asked as though she was talking to an abusive boss trying to build up her self esteem by talking down to their employees, "just pull the twine and destroy the gate?"

"As long as Barbara and Michelle can get through it safely," Faith said in a calm and even manner.

"Barbara's not going to be able to step over this," Jordi whined.

"You're not a baby, Jordi," Faith whined back, "figure it out."

"What happened to 'we're doing this together,'" Jordi asked.

"It feels like I'm doing this alone," Faith said, "good luck Jordi, I'm going to go care for Michelle."

Jordi knitted her brows together as she watched her emotional support person turn her back on her. She felt a sense of anger, both at Faith and at herself for being so helpless. She knew she couldn't do everything alone, she just didn't know what it was she could do and everyone seemed angry at her. Was it really her fault she needed so much help? No one was mad at Michelle for being dependent, so why were they mad at her?

Jordi pulled the twine apart and yanked the wood planks out of their hold. Her anger making the chore light work, she tossed all the bits into the garden of lost things.

"There," Jordi said with great satisfaction, "we can all walk through that now."

She went back inside to find Faith holding Michelle's head, trying to give her some water.

"What are you doing?" Jordi asked, in shock.

"She might be too tired to drink," Faith said.

"She might be sleeping."

"She's always sleeping, and she needs water."

"Is she swallowing?" Jordi asked.

"Of course she is," Faith said, watching Michelle's throat for movement, "I'm not trying to waterboard the girl."

Jordi tipped herself over the side of the empty couch and lay on her back.

"We did good work today," Jordi said.

"That's good," Faith said, putting the drink down and laying Michelle's head back on the pillow.

"I'm going to rest for a bit now," Jordi said.

"Bowls is at three and you're already not giving the neighbours much time."

Jordi glared at her friend, "let me rest, Faith."

"Girl," Faith said, "you've been resting your whole life."

"No, I haven't," Jordi said sitting up, a wave of heat and adrenaline thrashing through her body.

Jordi folded her arms and glared up towards the ceiling, she counted all the cracks she could see to try help her regulate her own emotions.

"Tell me when you're ready," Faith said in a calm, soft voice.

Jordi got up from the couch and with clenched fists, stormed downstairs into her basement. She threw open the door that had once led into her sanctuary. She used to open up the door to see her unused pool table, her overused couch and the wonderfully large television. Today she opened the door and saw an empty room with bits of wallpaper and plaster all over the ground. The emptiness of the room matched how Jordi felt in the pit of her stomach. She recalled the safety and comfort she felt from her familiar room. Her safe space.

Now she looked at four walls. Four walls with a roof. It wasn't hers anymore. Someone else had claimed it and put fear into her. She felt lost and angry and sad and scared and vulnerable all at the same time. Someone had walked into her sanctuary and taken her peace. She had no where she could go and recharge, she had nowhere that was hers.

Jordi closed the door and walked back upstairs.

"I'm ready now," Jordi said.

Faith puffed out her chest, "do you wanna check if Barbara needs lunch first?"

"What's the point?" Jordi said, "we act like doing all of this is going to fix everything. Nothing is going to fix what happened. The police aren't going to fix what happened. Barbara won't fix what happened. I can't fix what happened."

"No one's asking you to," Faith said.

Jordi turned on her sad and lonely heel to go check on Barbara.

Jordi didn't knock this time, she walked through the door and found Barbara sitting up, playing with her hair.

"Oh," Barbara looked surprised, "you didn't knock."

"Do I have to?" Jordi asked with an edge to her voice.

"I would expect it out of politeness," Barbara said.

"Can I talk to you?" Jordi asked.

Barbara's whole demeanor softened, "of course, what's wrong?"

Barbara moved to the bed and put her arm out for Jordi to sit next to her. Jordi sat, allowing Barbara's hand to hover above her shoulder.

Billy T. James swaggered over and trampled on top of Jordi's lap to settle into a sweet ball of fluff on top of Barbara. Barbara took her hand away from Jordi and placed it on top of her favourite cloud.

"I think it's time the furniture was replaced downstairs," Jordi said.

"Pardon?" Barbara asked.

"I think I need a proper place to sleep," Jordi said with a glum face.

"It has been quite a shock," Barbara said, "but that's not something I can do right now."

"Why not?"

"We can't let someone walk all over us and then tell them it's perfectly okay and just carry on as normal," Barbara explained, "If we replace everything it's like saying we don't even care about what happened. We must learn from these situations and grow stronger." Jordi looked at her great-aunt, "but I have nowhere to sleep."

"You did fine last night," Barbara said, "we must wait to hear from the Police and they will tell us what they think we should do."

"I can't play my game," Jordi said, "I can't relax."

"I'm sorry to hear you miss your game," Barbara said with a hint of sternness, "but that is no reason to let someone else win. We will not roll over."

"I don't understand," Jordi said, "I'm sure you have enough money to replace everything and buy better locks."

"That's not the point," Barbara said. She put a hand around Jordi's shoulders, "we can cope with this for now and we will get everything back once the investigation is complete-"

"There was no investigation."

"The Police are investigating it now and will contact us when they've found the person who did this."

"You think?" Jordi asked.

"I do think," Barbara said, "for now, we just have to be strong and take care of each other."

Barbara looked at her young dependant, "we must stay strong, stay positive, do what we can to stay happy until we've gotten through these tough times."

"Yeah, alright," Jordi said, feeling dejected, "I just don't think today is the right day for a party."

"What do you mean?" Barbara asked.

"I just think that with everything going on, we should postpone your birthday and see how we feel once all of this is over," Jordi said.

Barbara took a long, deep breath in.

"Don't you think?" Jordi asked, "I could go stay at Michelle's and look after her. You could stay here with a carer, maybe? And then I'll come back once everything is sorted and I'll throw you a birthday party then, promise."

Barbara steeled herself as she tried to speak in a calm manner, "what I have said to you still stands, Jordan." She took in a breath.

"If you leave, you are not coming back."

"What do you mean?" Jordi asked.

"You are still on your last straw," Barbara said, "just because we had a traumatic event occur, does not mean the slate is wiped clean."

Jordi looked at Barbara with pitiful eyes.

"You are still to care for me," Barbara's voice rose in anger, "I still expect this house to be cared for, I still expect food to go on the table, I still expect that garden to be turned into what one would actually call a garden, and I do expect a birthday party. Thank you very much."

Jordi looked at Barbara with astonishment and a hint of fear.

"I think the thing we need most at a time like this is a little bit of joy and I do expect to have my friends gathered around me and for there to be cake, and snacks, and drinks, and a lot of laughter. If you disagree, I can call my sister today."

Barbara closed her eyes and red flowed to her cheeks and forehead.

"I'm sure you don't feel like it, Jordan, but with everything that has gone on, I believe it is the least you could do," Barbara kept her eyes closed and pursed her lips, "you should leave my room now."

"But I was going to offer you lunch."

"Leave. Now."

Chapter 12

"I'm not doing anything for her, ever again," Jordi stormed into the sitting room.

"What happened?" Faith asked.

"She's mean, she's rude, she's selfish," Jordi lay face down on the couch.

"Woah, that's a turn around," Faith said, "what did she do? Did she say something?"

"She's not buying me anything," Jordi whined into a pillow.

"What?" Faith asked, full of judgement.

Jordi hit the couch cushion with her fists three times and then sat up on her knees, "I asked her, very politely, if I could go stay at Michelle's to help take care of her- she needs help, look at her." Jordi let tears fall towards her cracked lips.

"I asked her if I could stay at Michelle's while she bought me some new furniture so I had somewhere to sleep and she said no."

Jordi began to heave as more tears fell down her cheeks.

"I said I didn't think now was a good time to focus on a party with everything we've been through but she said

I have to fix everything and throw her the best birthday party she's ever had or I'm not welcome in her home anymore."

Jordi let the heaving take over and allowed the hyperventilation to overtake her body. Faith sat up on the couch next to Jordi and wrapped her up in a big hug.

"I'm so sorry you're in this situation," Faith said, "but I kind of agree with Barbara."

"I know you do but you don't have to say it," Jordi said, pulling out of the hug.

"I mean," Faith shrugged, "you have been kind of lazy and just because this has happened doesn't mean you can get what you want and expect Barbara to be okay with it."

"I have needs too," Jordi said, "not just Barbara."

"Of course you do," Faith said, "but your responsibility is to take care of Barbara and she needs you now more than ever."

Jordi didn't know what to say. She felt anger towards her friend for going against her but she could feel her demeanor softening as she understood Faith was right, Barbara did need her.

"She just has a long list of demands," Jordi said, calmer now.

"And what do we do when we have a long list?" Faith asked in a patronising tone.

"We talk to our friends like they're babies?" Jordi asked.

"Yes we do," Faith said as though she was talking to a baby or a fluffy animal, "yes we do ittle, wittle munchkin."

"Stop it," Jordi said, "I get it, I can just walk myself through it. You don't have to treat me like a child."

"Let's get onto those neighbours," Faith suggested.

Jordi stood herself up from the couch, "alright then. But what's the plan?"

Faith gave Jordi the most death defying side eye, "It's your job to come up with the plan, Jordan."

"Ew, don't call me that," Jordi said.

"I will when I want to," Faith replied.

Jordi groaned, "I guess we just knock on their door."

"How do we get past their gates?" Faith asked.

"So many questions, Faith," Jordi said.

"Jordi, you have to think," Faith said.

"We call them on their gate phone and we ask that way," Jordi shrugged.

"People around here have gate phones?" Faith asked, surprised, "that's so fancy."

"Yeah," Jordi said.

"Cool, let's execute this plan," Faith threw on her shoes and stood at the door, "Jordi, hurry up."

Jordi slumped her shoulders and shoved her feet inside her shoes, "let's go," she groaned.

Faith and Jordi walked along the path she had created that morning all the way to the street.

They made it to the top of the driveway and looked out. Arney Road stood still. The road was paved without a single bump or stone out of place. The pavement was silky smooth and the sun softly glowed down on all the homes.

"First one," Faith skipped over to Jordi's next door neighbour.

The hedge covered the house for privacy and the only thing Jordi and Faith could see was luscious green. Jordi looked down the long driveway protected by a towering black gate with cherubs on both corners.

"I think this is the gate phone," Faith said, pointing to a key pad, "how do you think we use it?"

"Dial?"

Faith pushed a series of numbers. Nothing happened. Faith pushed "1" and waited.

"Who's there?" A voice from the keypad said.

"My name is Faith and we want to talk-"

"Who's there?" The voice said again.

"There's a button at the bottom," Jordi pointed at a numberless and colourless button at the bottom of the keypad. Faith held it down.

"My name is Faith and I want to talk to you about Barbara."

"Who?"

"Faith. My name is Faith. Jordi is your neighbour," Faith said, holding down the numberless button.

"Which neighbour?"

"Jordi?" Faith said.

"Don't know them."

"And Barbara. She's dying and it's her birthday today," Faith explained.

Jordi gave her friend a hard whack on the shoulder.

"I'm really sorry to hear that," The voice said.

"Can we invite you to her party at The Remuera Club today?" Faith asked.

"No thank you," The voice said, "you need to leave now."

"Have you ever met them?" Faith asked, releasing the numberless and colourless button.

Jordi shook her head.

"Good," said Faith, "they're rude."

"Yeah," agreed Jordi.

"Next house?" Faith asked.

Jordi shrugged.

The next house had a long, steep driveway and no gate. There was no keypad like the last house.

"It looks steep," Jordi said.

"Nice view, though," Faith said looking out past the driveway onto the slither of shimmering ocean she could see.

"I bet it's spectacular down there."

"Should we go down?" Faith asked.

"What?" Jordi exclaimed, "down there? That's somebody's house."

"Isn't that the point?" Faith asked.

"What if they don't know Barbara?" Jordi asked.

"I thought you said everyone knew Barbara."

Jordi looked down at her feet, "I mean. I thought maybe they might."

"Let's go down and ask," Faith took Jordi's hand and led her down the long driveway.

Faith and Jordi saw two teenage girls with curly hair picking pebbles off the wall lining the driveway.

"Who are you?" One of them asked.

"We want to know if you know Barbara?" Faith asked.

One of the girls shrugged, "Mum's in there," the girl pointed at a three story house with glass windows instead of walls.

A middle aged woman walked out the door and up to the two young girls like a bodyguard protecting their precious jewels.

"Hello," The woman said, placing her hands on each of the teenage girls shoulders, "can I help you?"

"Do you know Barbara?" Faith asked.

"No," the woman said.

"She's my grandmother," Jordi said.

"I'm afraid I don't know you either," the woman smiled without a single drop of kindness in her eyes, "whatever you're selling, we're not buying."

"She's sick and old and it's her birthday today," Jordi rambled.

"Tell her happy birthday."

"We're throwing her a birthday party this afternoon at The Remuera Club," Jordi said. "Everyone's playing bowls and I was wondering- we were wondering if you wanted to come?" Jordi asked, "It's her 80th."

The woman looked down at her two kids. They both looked disgruntled and annoyed.

"I think that would be lovely," the woman smiled with just an ounce of kindness in her eyes, "we would love to come and celebrate Betty."

"Barbara," Jordi corrected.

"I'm so sorry," the woman said, "we would love to come and celebrate Barbara. What should we bring?"

"Nothing," Jordi said, "see you at The Club at three."

"We will see you at three," the woman waved as Faith and Jordi turned around and ran back up the driveway.

"That was so scary," Jordi puffed with her hands on her thighs, "but we did it."

"We did it," Faith picked up one of Jordi's hands and high-fived it. Jordi let herself fall onto the ground. She sat there as she waited for her breathing to slow.

"That was great," Faith jumped up in enthusiasm, "can you stand?" She asked, reaching her hand out for Jordi to grab.

"Yeah," Jordi wheezed as she used Faith's hand to help steady her as she stood back up.

"Next house," Faith said.

"No," Jordi puffed.

"It wasn't that bad," Faith said.

Jordi shook her head, "It was terrible."

"But it was a success," Faith said in confusion.

"One more house," Jordi said in defeat.

Faith clapped her hands in excitement and skipped over to the next house which had a solid wooden gate and a keypad off to the side, with a screen above it. Faith pressed the button with a picture of a phone on it. Jordi walked over and stood in front of the camera, her breathing now normal.

"Who is it?" A gruff female voice asked. Faith and Jordi could see themselves on the gate phone screen.

"We would like to invite you to Barbara's birthday today at-"

"Barbara?" The voice asked.

"She's my grandmother and she's sick-"

"Okay?" The voice asked.

"She's your neighbour and-"

"I'm aware."

"What?" Jordi said.

"I'm aware, go on."

Jordi thought for a second, "It's her birthday today, we're hosting it at The Remuera Club, we're-"

"She's a Bitch," the voice said. The call disconnected and the screen went black.

"Who made them have a bad day?" Faith asked.

"Hang on, my phone's vibrating."

Faith watched as Jordi pulled her phone out of her pocket and stared at the screen with disgust and embarrassment.

"Why is Michelle calling me?" Jordi answered, "Are you dying?"

"Sorry," Michelle said, "how much longer will you be? Barbara keeps ringing her bell."

"Not long, promise," Jordi said, hanging up.

"She okay?" Faith asked.

"She's fine. What now?"

"Should we try another one?" Faith asked.

"Do you want to?" Jordi looked at her in confusion, "I don't think this is working. I just wish I knew where her friends lived."

"I think this is the best you can do," Faith said, "what time is it?"

"One."

"Do we need to start getting ready?" Faith asked, "And getting Barbara ready for the party?"

"Oh, it's not a real party," Jordi sent a kick towards the ground, "why can't I do anything right?"

"Let's go home and have something to eat," Faith suggested.

"No," Jordi said, "If we go home, we have to face Barbara and her stupid bell. That would be even worse."

Faith looked at her friend with pity.

"You promised Michelle you'd be back soon."

"You're right, we have one person coming already, maybe that's enough," Jordi said, she felt a wave of motivation blow over her with the breeze, "maybe I can go home and face Barbara."

"Home?" Faith asked.

"Home," Jordi repeated, "we can count this as a win, I guess."

"We're doing what we can," Faith agreed, "we'd better run," Faith began to jog.

"Wait!" Jordi called, falling behind immediately. She stumbled but ran as fast as she could.

Faith looked behind her, "legs up, chest high, nose to the air. You got this, keep going."

Jordi pulled her chest up and kept running as fast as she could. Faith came to her side and jogged next to her.

"Keep going, Jordi," Faith yelled as she clapped her hands, "knees up, chest up, run."

Jordi ran and puffed and ran and puffed until she reached her driveway one hundred metres up the road. She bent over with her hands on her thighs in front of Barbara's front door.

"Breathe," Faith yelled.

"Geez," Jordi puffed.

"Please give me a Google review," Faith said.

"You have enough of those," Jordi said, "I can see why your clients like you, that was actually weirdly encouraging."

Faith smiled a proud smile, "let's go inside and get your grandmother ready."

Jordi agreed.

They walked inside and saw Michelle sitting up on the couch.

"Michelle, are you feeling better?" Faith said with her chest puffed out like a bird attracting a mate.

Michelle moved her head down, then up as though she was nodding through a pile of dense mud.

"I'm going to go get Barbara ready," Jordi said.

"Do we need a cake?" Faith asked.

Jordi stopped short.

"A cake," Faith re-stated, "And some food and drinks, unless they provide that at the club?"

Jordi stood frozen.

"And what if Barbara doesn't like bowls, are there any back up games?" Faith asked.

"Faith," Jordi said slowly, "you are uninvited," she walked with confidence out of the sitting room.

Jordi walked into Barbara's bedroom without knocking, "hello, grandmother."

Barbara was sitting up in the middle of the room with her legs crossed and her eyes closed.

"Ah, yes, Jordan," Barbara gave a soft nod, "welcome, I was just meditating and I couldn't get myself up."

"Are you ready for your party?"

"My party?" Barbara asked, "today?"

"Of course."

"Oh, Jordan, you are too kind," Barbara went to uncross her legs but found it hard to move. "Could you help me?"

"We have to go," Jordi said, watching her great-aunt struggle.

"Just a moment, Jordan," Barbara said with annoyance, "I am a bit older than you."

"Sorry," Jordi said, looking down at her feet.

Barbara managed to straighten her legs but then slouched in defeat, "could you help me, Jordan?"

Jordi went over to her great-aunt. She crouched down and placed her hands underneath her great-aunts right arm. Her skin felt soft and fragile, bones thin and Jordi reckoned she would be able to fit her index finger and thumb around Barbara's entire wrist with room to spare.

"When you're ready, I'm here," Jordi said, "just lean on me."

Barbara nodded, "thank you."

Barbara leaned on Jordi who helped lift her up enough so she was able to sit on her knees and from there place one foot on the floor and then the other. With help she stood up.

"Thank you, Jordan," Barbara said as she patted her pretend grand-daughter on the shoulder.

"How quickly can you get ready?" Jordi asked.

"What time is the party?" Barbara asked.

"Three."

"Three?" Barbara asked, "Jordan, that's in about half an hour."

"That's ok," Jordi said, "It's your party, you can show up at any time you wish."

"Alright, Jordan," Barbara said, "give me some time to have a shower and put a dress on." Barbara's arms wobbled as she detached herself from Jordi.

"You don't have to," Jordi said, "you look perfect as you are."

"Jordan, don't tease," Barbara said.

"No, really," Jordi said, "we'll be playing bowls and you look perfect for that."

"You are so lovely sometimes," Barbara said, "shall we go then?"

Jordi nodded. Barbara slipped her arm through Jordi's.

"Alright," Jordi said, "I'll take you to the car and then I'll get the others."

"Who are the others?" Barbara asked, taking careful steps.

"Faith and Michelle," Jordi said.

"Ah, yes," Barbara said, "do you know where the wheelchair is?"

"We have a wheelchair?" Jordi asked.

"Yes," Barbara confirmed, "I was wondering if it might be best that you use that to help me to the car."

"Maybe," Jordi said, "Where is it?"

"It's folded up, in the cupboard by the stairs," Barbara said.

"Which stairs?" Jordi asked.

"Oh, Jordan," Babara was quiet for a moment, "I'm not sure of that answer."

"I think you'll be okay," Jordi said, "I'll hold onto you."

"Okay," Barbara patted Jordi's arm with her free hand. The two of them walked slowly and cautiously towards the front door, passing through the sitting room and out through the garden, through the space where the gate once was and into the Tesla.

"You sit here and I'll get the others," Jordi said, leaving the car door open for fresh air. She walked back into the house and into the sitting room, "guys, there's a wheelchair near the stairs, Michelle can use that to go out."

"Where's Barbara?" Faith asked.

"She's in the car."

"Jordi."

"The door is open, she's fine," Jordi said.

"Jordi, that's horrible," Faith said, "It's so hot outside."

"She's fine," Jordi said, "let's get Michelle in the car and then we can go to the party."

Faith ran out of the room and back into the room holding a black foldable wheelchair above her head.

"I've got it," Faith said, putting the chair down by the edge of the couch. That cupboard is the nicest storage room I have ever seen.

"Thanks," Jordi said, "It's all Barbara, she likes to waste space."

"Michelle, can you get in the wheelchair, do you think?" Faith asked.

Michelle once again moved her head down and then back up as though she was lifting her head out of a stormy ocean. She looked to the edge of the couch but did not move.

"Let's lift her," Faith said, putting her hands underneath Michelle's armpits and shuffling her into the wheelchair.

"Now we just have to get her to the car."

Faith took charge of pushing the wheelchair while Jordi walked in front and moved aside all furniture, doors, twigs, stones, leaves, and branches that could hinder the smooth ride in the chair.

Barbara turned her head and saw the three of them coming towards the car. She stood up, holding onto the scalding hot door frame for support.

"I thought that wheelchair was for me," Barbara said to Jordi. Her face had angry tears piercing her eyes.

"Sorry, Barbara," Jordi said, "Michelle needs it more. Can she sit in the front?"

"I guess I'll sit in the middle at the back then?" Barbara asked.

"Thanks," Jordi said, keeping her focus on her friends. In a huff, Barbara moved to the back door of the car and sat down in her new designated seat. "Who knew I would pay for all of these things just to end up sitting in the back seat," she said to no one in particular.

Faith and Jordi lifted Michelle into the front seat as best they could, Faith doing most of the work. Michelle landed on the seat in the car but was tipped over by Jordi's lack of spatial awareness.

"You pushed her," Faith accused.

"Sorry, Michelle," Jordi said, looking guilty.

Michelle pushed herself up and adjusted herself into a sitting position but her face looked tired and drained.

"Faith, you're in the back seat," Jordi said, walking around to the driver's side of the car.

"Can you open the door?" Faith asked.

Jordi pushed a button and a door handle appeared for Faith to open the door herself.

"Thanks," Faith said.

Jordi started the car and did a U-turn out of the driveway.

"Wait," Jordi said, slamming the brakes. Faith and Barbara flew forward, their seatbelt the only thing stopping them from smashing themselves into the back of the front seats.

"The wheelchair," Jordi flew out of the car and into the driveway, "It's gone."

"Idiot," Faith shouted out the window, "I put it in the car already."

"Oh," Jordi sat back down.

"Drive carefully, Jordi," Faith scolded.

Jordi didn't say anything. She continued driving out of the driveway and down the street towards The Remuera Club. She parked on the street behind a shiny white Tesla that looked just like theirs.

"We're here," Jordi said.

"I'll get the wheelchair," Faith jumped out of the car and pulled the wheelchair from the boot. "Barbara, are you okay to get out on your own?"

Barbara had been silent the entire car ride and her eyebrows had knitted together in anger. She didn't say anything, she just nodded.

Faith slid out of the car, kicking the door open.

Barbara managed to push herself up off the seat and into a standing position as Faith guided Michelle into the wheelchair. Barbara watched as this twenty year old was being waited on hand and foot while she, eighty, was being asked to do everything on her own.

"Do you want me to push her?" Barbara asked with distaste.

"No, it's fine," Jordi said, taking the handlebars.

"You can lean on me," Faith said, slipping her arm through Barbara's, "Jordi's going to take Michelle and go inside and check everything is ready, aren't you Jordi?"

"Yeah," Jordi said, walking ahead.

Chapter 13

Jordi walked into the orange, cork coloured hall and saw four strips of green rolled out in lines. There were people in their eighties, young families, and teenagers all playing bowls or helping themselves to tea and biscuits set up on a long table underneath the noticeboard.

"Can I help you?" A woman in jean shorts and a white top asked.

"My grandmother and some friends would like to play bowls," Jordi said.

"Have you booked?" The woman asked.

"I don't think so, but my grandmother is a member of this club," Jordi explained.

"That's nice," The woman said, "but you have to book if you want to play."

"We were told you don't have to book," Jordi whined, "And it's her birthday."

"Did you book the hall for her birthday?" The woman asked.

"No," Jordi said.

"Did you book a lane?" The woman asked.

"No."

The woman shrugged, "Not much I can do."

"Do you sell cake?" Jordi asked.

"Cake?" The woman said, "we have pavlova on the menu but it's only a piece."

"That could work," Jordi said, "where can we eat it?"

"There are tables outside," the woman said, "how many pieces do you want?"

"Four," Jordi said.

"Sit down and I'll bring them over to you," the woman walked away.

Jordi walked out to her friends and Barbara, "we can have a seat outside to enjoy your cake."

"Oh, Jordan," Barbara said, "you shouldn't have."

"Of course," Jordi said, all high pitched and uncomfortable.

The only table outside that could fit all five of them was under a blossom tree that wasn't blooming. The green leaves were thick and covered them from the harsh sunlight in the middle of the Auckland summer.

"Here you are," Jordi said, pulling out a chair for Barbara.

Barbara took a seat in the plastic white chair with a bird poo stain in the corner. The chair was on uneven ground and tipped back 3cm as Barbara sat into it. The table matched the chairs with the white plastic and bird poo stains in the corners and all down the legs of the table. There was a circular hole right in the middle, fit for an umbrella that was nowhere to be seen.

Faith removed one of the chairs and pushed Michelle right up to the table's edge.

"Looks nice," Faith said, taking a seat, "we have some lovely shade, this is nice."

"This will look beautiful in the spring," Faith said, looking up.

"Be careful looking up," Barbara said, "there is evidence of bird life."

"That's lovely," Faith said.

"Oh yes, it is," Barbara said, "until you get a dropping on your head."

"Four Pavlova's," a different woman in jean shorts and a white top said. She placed them down in the middle of the table. Faith leaned across and passed them to each individual person.

"I'll bring you some spoons," the woman in jean shorts said.

"This is the cake?" Barbara asked. Her pitch was high and she tried to smile but the corners of her mouth didn't quite turn up.

"Are we not singing 'Happy Birthday'?" Faith asked.

"Let's sing it now," Jordi said, "Happy Birthday to you!" They all joined in, except Michelle, and sang at the top of their lungs. Michelle's mouth moved but no sound came out.

"That was lovely," Barbara said, as she picked up her spoon from the tray of cutlery that had been left in the centre of the table during their song, "let's all dig in and enjoy."

"It's delicious," Faith said, taking a bite.

"It is good," Jordi agreed.

"It's wonderful," Barbara said, "thank you, Jordan." Michelle took a tired hand and picked up the spoon, making her hand shake. The weight of the thin metal felt like a one hundred and seventy kg weight. She let the spoon fall into the pavlova and took a weary bite. The sweet, soft dessert was easy to swallow, but she placed the spoon back down on the dirty table letting her hand rest and fall to her side. She let out a sigh and leant back in her chair.

"She doesn't look well," Barbara commented.

"She's not," Jordi said.

"When is everyone arriving?" Barbara asked.

"They're inside," Jordi said.

"They're inside?" Barbara asked.

"Yes."

"Then why are we sitting out here, shouldn't we go in and say hello?"

"They'll come out, I'm sure," Jordi said, "I thought this was some nice quality time and if you're not up to going in there, you don't have to."

"We've come all this way," Barbara said.

"Barbara," a deep, gruff voice said from behind her. Barbara turned around and saw a woman around her age with wide shoulders, short shaven grey hair and a pearl necklace around her neck.

"Hello," Barbara said.

"I was told they were celebrating your birthday today," The woman said, standing over Barbara like a looming shadow.

"Yes," Barbara affirmed with no emotion in her voice, "these are my grandchildren, we were just having some cake."

"Interesting," the woman eyed Jordi and her friends, "they don't look like your grandchildren."

Barbara sat up straight, "that's because you've never met them. So you wouldn't know what they look like."

The woman walked around the table and took the spare seat near Michelle's wheelchair and sat down on it.

"Excuse me, but I'm trying to have a lovely afternoon with my grandchildren," Barbara said, "you may move on and join the party inside."

"I'm more than happy sitting out here," the woman said, "I feel like it would be nice to catch up."

"There is no need," Barbara said.

"There is all the need," the woman stated, "I want to meet your grandchildren."

"You can meet them later," Barbara said.

"Now," the woman used her eyes to stab into Barbara's soul.

"Please leave," Barbara said.

"Alright," the woman said, giving up and removing herself from the plastic chair, "I'll see you inside, I guess," she stood up and went inside the hall.

"That voice sounded familiar," Faith said, "does she live near your house, Barbara?"

"A few doors down," Barbara said.

Jordi and Faith looked at each other.

"Do you know her?" Jordi asked.

"We have a bit of a history," Barbara said, "we've been neighours for years."

"They don't seem very nice," Faith said, taking another bite of her pavlova.

"There's some history," Barbara said again. She also took another bite of pavlova.

"What kind of history?" Faith asked.

Barbara gestured to her chewing to signal she couldn't talk.

"Should we be scared of her?" Jordi asked, "Is it something illegal?"

"Jordan," Barbara scolded with her mouth full. She placed her spoon down on her plate, "how could you suggest something like that?"

"Sorry," Jordi looked down at her plate of pavlova with cream and berries.

"It is nothing now and nothing any of you need to worry about," Barbara said, "but I am surprised she is here."

"Who is she?" Faith asked, "what's her name?"

Barbara let out a deep sigh, "she used to be an old friend but we went our separate ways." Barbara took another bite of pavlova, "we were partners. In business and in life but..." She said more to herself than anyone else. Flecks of Pavlova protruded from her mouth as she spoke.

"But what?" Faith asked, leaning forward, "can you tell us?"

"Nothing any of you kids need to worry about," Barbara said again.

"But she's here, so maybe we should know," Jordi said.

"And why do we need to pretend to be your grandkids?" Faith asked.

Barbara let out another sigh, "we would enjoy each other's company in a way that was frowned upon in my day."

Jordi and Faith leant in. Michelle attempted to take another bite of her pavlova.

"We did everything together, including starting a business. It was fun until one day it wasn't and I decided it was best to sell up and join a bigger company," Barbara said again, "I also told her I wanted to start a family."

"But you had a business all my life," Jordi said.

"Yes. The job didn't last long, so I decided to branch out and start my own property management business once again," Barbara let that sit, "without her this time."

"But she was your girlfriend," Jordi sat back in astonishment.

"We meant a lot to each other. She said she would give up her family and her future for me," Barbara said, "I just wasn't ready to do the same."

"She was going to give up her family for you?" Faith asked.

"She did," Barbara said, "In those days people were more open about being unaccepting. It was more the norm."

"Did you stay single after that?" Faith asked, "why did you not get back together?"

"I wanted a family and I tried," Barbara let her hands shake as she sat back in her plastic, flimsy chair, "but men are just not for me."

"And you didn't want to get back with her after that?" Faith asked.

Barbara let out a quiet laugh, "after what happened to the business, she would never have me."

"What happened to the business?" Faith questioned.

"I sold it," Barbara said matter-of-factly.

"Would she get back with you if you talked to her?" Faith asked, "she did come to your party today."

"I suppose," Barbara said, "but she acted like I did something terrible and I don't know if she'll ever get over herself."

"I don't understand," Faith said.

"I sold the original business without her full permission."

"Oh dear," Faith said, "why did you do that?"

"Money," Barbara answered.

"Was there a lot of money in the business?" Faith asked.

"No," Barbara shook her head, "It sold for next to nothing. I moved to one real estate company and poor old Elizabeth went to another to pay off our bills."

"Do you think that's why she was mad?" Faith asked.

"Oh no," Barbara said, "I'm sure she would've jumped at the chance to be my business partner again but I never asked her. I think that's what has got her bonnet in a twist. That and she still loves me, probably."

"That's really sad," Faith said, "I'm sorry to hear about all this."

"Oh yes," Barbara said, "then I told her one of my children had found me an employee."

"But you don't have any children," Jordi stated.

Faith swung her head towards Jordi.

Barbara lent across the table and hissed, "don't you ever say something like that again. That was the one thing I could hold over Elizabeth's head."

"You're not," Faith pointed at Barbara and Jordi, "wait, you two aren't…"

"We're family," Barbara said, "And I don't want any of this dirty laundry getting out in the open. This is completely private. Not that I said anything about anything."

"How did she think you had a kid if you didn't?" Faith asked.

"Oh," Barbara waved her hand as though she could wave away the thought like an indecent smell, "I told her it was a long lost child I gave up in my teens who finally found me. She never suspected a thing."

Barbara pushed her chair away from the table, stood up, and hobbled towards the entrance to the inside of the hall.

"She's not your grandmother?" Faith asked.

"She's my great-aunt," Jordi explained.

"My baby!" Maggie shouted, throwing her arms wide. She ran over to Michelle and wrapped her arms around her daughter, "how are you? Are you okay? Why do you look worse?"

"Hey Maggie," Jordi said.

"Hello, love," Maggie said, "how has my baby been?"

"Good," Faith said, "she got better and cooked us all dinner."

Maggie took a step back and looked at her daughter in the wheelchair.

"But now she looks like this," Faith said, glum, "but she's eating the pavlova."

"Good girl," Maggie said, "I'm sure the sugar will help with a bit of energy. Where did the wheelchair come from?"

"It's Barbara's," Jordi explained.

"Oh, how nice of her to let Michelle use it," Maggie's eyes went all watery, "I had better go and thank her." Maggie gave Michelle another squeeze before she wandered inside the hall.

Maggie walked inside and saw happy families all surrounding lines of green and cheering each other on as balls rolled along the floor, hitting other balls. Cheers and groans were heard echoing throughout the indoors. Maggie saw young mums with their daughters jumping up and down and laughing. She saw children running up and down, around the hall. She watched a group of teenagers chatting away at the snack table. She stared at a couple in their twenties, one of the women stood on her tip-toes as she measured herself against her partner. They smiled at each other before turning back to watch the family game of bowls.

"Barbara," Maggie said, "thank you so much for letting my daughter use your wheelchair. As a mum, it means so much to me to see other people taking care of her like this. She usually can't move far from her bed when she has these episodes. It really means the world."

"Oh, that's not a problem," Barbara said, "your daughter means a lot to Jordan."

"Who's Jordan?" Maggie asked.

Barbara looked at Maggie with confusion.

"Oh, sorry, Jordi, yes," Maggie nodded, "she is lovely isn't she."

Barbara nodded, "when she wants to be."

"How has she been treating you lately?" Maggie asked.

"Oh, yes," Barbara said, "your daughter was enlisted to cook a lovely meal the other day and Jordan has tidied up a bit of the garden and brought me meals in bed, as asked."

"That sounds like Jordi," Maggie said, her voice soft and her eyes sparkling.

"I think I need to have her do a few more chores around the place. The light bulbs need replacing, I wouldn't mind new carpet, and that garden is horrendous," Barbara said.

Jordi waltzed into the hall, Faith followed behind pushing Michelle's chair.

"Everybody, I would like you to note it is a very special day today," Jordi said, projecting her voice across the hall, "my grandmother, Barbara, is celebrating her eightieth birthday today."

Faith sent her shoulders back and chest forward, she began singing 'Happy Birthday' in Opera.

Everyone started joining in but slowly fizzled out as they reached the sentence where you have to name the person who's having the birthday.

Jordi ran over to Barbara with a plate of biscuits and then jogged back to stand behind Faith as she finished her song on a vibrato.

Barbara gave a little smile and said, "I almost feel as though I should give Jordan her furniture back, but she has not learned her lesson."

She took a bite of a chocolate chip biscuit.

Chapter 14

Maggie looked at Barbara and felt the air whip across her cheeks. The imaginary whip along her face stung and the stabbing in her heart felt like a hole was being created to let her soul escape.

"What?" Maggie mumbled.

"Oh please," Barbara said, "you knew I had to do something."

Maggie now felt like someone was shoving her against a brick wall.

"You would do that to your own granddaughter?"

Barbara gave Maggie a sly look, "like you've never disciplined your daughter."

"On a much smaller scale, of course."

"This is nothing," Barbara said, "Jordan came to live with me to elevate her life, care for me, and create something big in the city. She's done nothing but hide in her cave. It's about time she learned the value of things."

"I agree Jordi has been given a lot with little expectation put on her, but she does do a lot. She's so young and doesn't know what she's doing-"

"You were that lost at twenty two?"

"We live in different times now," Maggie sighed, "Jordi just needs some guidance."

"I had no guidance at that age, did you?"

"Not so much but we had less options."

"Exactly, we had less to work with, unlike the young people today who get everything handed to them."

"Being handed something is one thing, handing out something and then taking it back is another."

"Oh, stop being so judgemental, you don't know what you're talking about."

"Treat her well, she's so young."

"Not so young anymore, I'm afraid," Barbara said, "at her age I was expected to be married with children."

Maggie looked over at Barbara and let a sense of sadness wash over her. The depth of her pain was felt in Maggie's gut, the desperate need to be validated and seen.

"You've done really well in your life, Barbara," Maggie said, "we see you and think you've done so well."

Barbara gave Maggie a glare as she fiddled with her top, "yes, well, that's enough."

Barbara thanked her guests as they left, sending her voice as far as ten metres in front of her. She walked over to Jordi and stood next to her as she turned and addressed the crowd, "this is my beautiful granddaughter, Jordan, who has a soul like an angel." Barbara opened her arms and gave Jordi a hug.

"Happy Birthday," someone shouted as all the bowls players kept playing. Some giggles rippled through the crowd.

Barbara took Jordi's hand and with a limp in her step, led her grand-niece over to a chair by the snack table. "Jordan," Barbara said, sitting down, "do I know anyone here?"

"Yeah, there's heaps of people you know," Jordi said, "they'll come and talk to you soon."

Barbara looked up at her grand-niece. Jordan looked as though standing was taking great effort. Every word coming out of her mouth looked as though she would need a week to recover from exertion. But Barbara remembered being in her early twenties and she knew all of that came easy. Barbara had been articulate, goal oriented and driven. At least in her mind. It was hard to be in your twenties but it didn't take as much effort as Jordan made it seem. Young Jordan, who had followed in her footsteps to leave the remote island of wine and start a life in the big city, had made a giant leap of faith but it felt as though that was all Jordan had in her. Barbara remembered when her family gifted her the house, she at least said 'thank you.'

Barbara let go of Jordan's hand and watched as her grand-niece re-joined her friends. How they chatted and checked on each other.

Barbara watched as Jordan chuckled and her cheeks gained colour and some sparkle entered her eyes.

She watched as her shoulders swayed along with the chatter and her knees jiggled. Jordan couldn't keep still even if her life depended on it.

"Oh Jordan," Barbara said under her breath. She waited patiently for almost an hour but nobody came to her for a chat or to wish her a happy birthday. She stood up from the seat and strolled over to her grand-niece.

"I'm afraid I'm not feeling very well and we must go back to the house," Barbara stated quietly to Jordi. Two teenage girls with curly brown hair ran past Barbara with fistfuls of chips and chocolate from the snack table.

"Of course," Jordi said. She slipped her soft, meaty arm underneath Barbara's soft, fragile skin. Barbara's arm had to be held out on a 45degree angle and she wasn't sure if this was helping or hindering her walking. Her arm ached as she held it to the side, wide enough to lean some weight onto Jordan. Her feet lifted and her body weight crashed into her shoes every time she placed her foot down and Jordi pulled her great-aunt along.

"Jordan, stop," Barbara scolded. Jordi turned and looked at her great-aunt who stood still, wearing a scowl.

"I thought you wanted to go," Jordi said.

"Slowly," Barbara said. She placed two hands around Jordi's arm with her smooth, soft, young skin.

They walked with careful steps back to the car.

"I shall like to sit in the front on the way home," Barbara stated.

"Michelle needs the front," Jordi said, "we won't be able to get her home otherwise."

Barbara took a deep breath in and felt the shake in her throat as the air went down. Her heart sank in her chest as she watched Jordi bend down to look Michelle in the eyes. She talked to her so softly and with such a sweet smile. Her bouncy curls dancing in the wind, full bodied with a deep, dark colour of brown; just like how Barbara's used to be. Jordan opened the front passenger door and with the help of her very fit friend, she moved Michelle to the front seat. Jordan moved Michelle's legs with such care, it brought tears to Barbara's eyes.

Barbara wasn't sure if these tears were jealousy or pride, she blinked them away into non-existence. She opened the door to the back seat and lowered herself in slowly. Her bones and blood felt as though it dropped as she sat. She pulled her legs into the car and squeezed them into the small gap left between her seat and Michelle's.

Barbara sat pressed up next to her grand-niece's friend for the duration of the car ride and felt she was on the wrong side of being fifteen again.

Jordan slammed the brakes once they reached the bottom of the driveway, sending Barbara's head forward, and her hands instinctively flew up to cover her head. She could hear a disapproving sigh from the front and caught a glimpse of Jordan's eyes looking her way.

As Jordan and her friends surrounded Michelle, Barbara took herself off towards what used to be her luscious entrance into her beautiful garden that was pruned, weeded and mown not a centimetre out of place. Now, she stepped over the fallen wood onto the flattened grass and stepped carefully past the fallen tree branches and leaves with threatening spikes. She reached the door and walked into her overheated house with bedding and clothes thrown all over her sitting room. She made her way to her bedroom with the soft-as-a-cloud carpet and the aircon sending a light breeze through her room. Billy T. James jumped up and wagged his tail as soon as Barbara entered. She sat on the bed and welcomed all the licks and excitable whines.

"At least someone loves me," Barbara said, giving Billy T. James a scratch behind the ear.

Barbara sat up in bed with her silk bathrobe around her and Billy T. James curled up at her hip. The picture frame on her wall doubled as a television and she played an episode of The Good Life. She laughed as she watched the Barbara on screen try to churn butter without success.

A light tapping was heard at her door.

Barbara turned the picture-frame-TV off and threw the bed covers over top of her. She lay her head down on the pillow and let out a cough.

"Come in," she said with a croak.

The door inched open and Jordan squeezed her head into the room before the rest of her body followed.

"Do you need anything?" Jordi asked.

"Maybe a cup of tea," Barbara said, croaking her voice even more, "oh, Jordan."

Barbara reached out a shaking hand from underneath the covers and Jordan took it in hers.

"Yes, Grandma," Jordi said.

Barbara felt the strength of young bones and held onto the capable hands which were there to help keep her sane.

"How are the gardens looking?" Barbara asked, "I would so love to be able to look out of the window in the morning and admire the beautiful flowers, it would aid so well in my recovery."

Jordan flung Barbara's hand towards the carpet. Barbara felt the hand she relied on let go and the pressure of gravity bent her wrist towards the carpet further than Barbara knew it could go.

"It's been a long day for me too, you can't keep asking me to do things," Jordi stomped her foot, shaking the room underneath Barbara, "didn't you like your birthday party?"

"You need to calm down, Jordan," Barbara said, bringing her hand back under the covers and rubbing her wrist.

"You seemed fine today when you thought we weren't looking," Jordi whispered.

"Excuse me?" Barbara asked, forgetting to croak. Jordan looked at her with nervousness in her eyes, "sorry. I just meant, I think you liked being around your friends."

"You and I both know there were no friends of mine there," Barbara stated.

"Well, I think you had a good time," Jordi said.

"I don't think that's up to you to decide how I feel," Barbara said.

"Sorry," Jordi said, looking down at the snow white carpet she had never cleaned in her life.

"I think you need to think about this and do a re-do for my actual birthday next weekend," Barbara said.

"What?" Jordi's head flew up and she looked at Barbara.

"We'll call this a practice round," Barbara said, "I understand you've been stressed so I can understand it's been hard to remember these small things."

Jordi fumed and it showed on her face like a billboard.

"Maybe instead of parties," Jordi shouted so loud Barbara's brain started to vibrate, "we focus on what we can do about the actual problem here, I have nowhere to sleep."

Jordi shook the room as she stormed out. The door slammed causing Barbara's heart to skip two beats in her chest. She lay back against her pillows, with a shaking hand, and restarted her show.

Jordan had not learned her lesson.

Two episodes later, another knock on the door was heard. A tough one, with purpose this time. Barbara paused her show and got herself and Billy T. James back under the covers.

"Yes?" She called.

"May I come in?" A gruff, female voice asked.

Barbara sat up. She remembered that voice from earlier. She got out of bed, slipped off her dressing gown, hiding it under her pillow. She walked into her walk-in closet and pulled out a bright yellow sun dress and slipped it over her head. She walked barefoot across her carpet and opened her door.

"Hello again," Barbara said, opening the door wide for her visitor.

"I thought I owed you a visit. A proper catch up," the woman said.

"It's been a while," Barbara acknowledged.

"It has," the woman walked over to Barbara's bed and took a seat, "I heard things aren't going well for you?"

"How so?"

"Health wise."

"Oh, yes," Barbara said, "what can one do at our age?"

"I thought I would pay you a visit," the gruff sounding woman said, "for old times sake."

Chapter 15

"How long has that woman been upstairs with your family member?" Faith asked.

"Just call her my grandmother," Jordi replied, "And, I don't know."

"Should we check on her?" Faith asked.

"No," Jordi said, "they'll be fine."

"I suppose they have history but what if something's wrong?" Faith asked, wringing her hands together.

"Nothing will be wrong," Jordi said lying back on the couch looking up at the sparkling white ceiling with subtle cracks all over the place.

"I'll show you out," Barbara said from another room. She walked with the gruff sounding woman out of the house and then back into the sitting room, alone.

"That was a long chat," Jordi said.

"Oh well, we did other things too," Barbara said, "we watched a bit of TV, had a nap, and she got to know Billy T. James a bit."

"You seem happy," Faith noted.

"It was a good catch up," Barbara said, "I feel a lot better now. I think she feels better too."

"Really?" Jordi asked.

"Yes. We might even rekindle our old friendship, who knows?" Barbara said, walking back across the sitting room, "I will need you to start on the gardens tomorrow, Jordan," Barbara said as she walked through the doorway.

"Who's helping me in the garden tomorrow?" Jordi asked.

"I'm afraid I have to go back to work tomorrow, I can't stay any longer," Faith explained.

"But what about Michelle?" Jordi asked.

Faith looked at Michelle who was asleep on the couch. Her skin seemed to get more and more pale each time Faith looked at her.

"I suppose I could get the week off," Faith contemplated, looking at her sick friend.

"She needs you, Faith," Jordi said.

"You need me," Faith corrected.

"I can take care of myself," Jordi said.

"No, you can't," Faith scoffed.

"Yes, I can."

"No, you can't."

"Yes, I can."

"No-"

"Stop it," Michelle growled with all the energy she could conjure.

"I'm going to work, then," Faith said, "since you can look after yourself so well."

"Go," Jordi said, folding her arms, "see if I care."

"I will," Faith grabbed her hand bag, "tell Barbara she can keep Billy T. James for as long as she needs." Faith turned on her heel, her hair flew around her as hair does in dramatic situations and she marched out the door.

The next morning Jordi awoke with panic in her chest. She was alone to care for Barbara and Michelle. She had her long list of chores that needed to be completed and two people completely dependent on her.

"I have to clean the garden today," Jordi said to Michelle who didn't respond, "I can do this, just one step at a time."

Jordi picked up her phone and began writing a list: Clean garden. She wrote.

"No, that's too big of a job," Jordi said to a sleeping Michelle, "I just have to break it down."

She wrote: 1) Go outside.

"That's achievable," Jordi said with a burst of enthusiasm, "Michelle, will you be okay if I pop outside for a bit, do you need anything?"

Michelle didn't respond. Jordi placed an ear up to her mouth, "breathing, good. I'll be quick."

Jordi stood outside in the garden looking out at the overgrown grass, the green tentacles tickled her waist as she stepped into the tangled abyss.

"I guess I have to start somewhere," she reached down to the roots of the grass and yanked. The grass locked itself into the dirt and Jordi fell over backwards hitting something hard.

"The lawnmower?" Jordi said, turning around and seeing a lawnmower shaped grass sculpture behind her. She rubbed her head with one hand as she pulled the weeds apart with the other. The weeds had been covering up brown rust which was falling off with the vines. Jordi yanked the grass away until the entire crumbly sculpture had been uncovered.

She pulled the lawnmower onto the the path she had cleared earlier and felt a layer of rust fall off into her palm.

Jordi stamped her feet through the overgrown grass to find more goodies hiding.

"What's that?" Jordi asked nobody with excitement. She pulled weeds away from what turned into a tree stump. She ran around the garden looking for lumps of weeds and pulling them away to discover hidden treasure. By the time she was finished, she had found three bird baths, a table, seven chairs, a full length mirror, a rabbit sculpture, seven gnomes, and a CD player.

The grass was all trampled on and flat, which, in Jordi's book, was similar to mowing.

She trampled her way up to Barbara.

She knocked and was called into the room.

"The garden has been flattened," Jordi said from the doorway, "you can see outside."

"I do see outside, and you did a wonderful job," Barbara said with the seriousness of a funeral.

"Are you happy?" Jordi asked.

"I am pleased with the work you have done," Barbara said, "but I have some bad news."

Jordi walked to Barbara's side, "Are you okay?"

"I'm afraid, Elizabeth, who you met, was not here to be friendly," Barbara said, "she is trying to repossess this house."

"What do you mean?" Jordi asked.

"She is currently trying to take our house."

"How can she do that when it's not hers?" Jordi asked.

"She claims it's already in her name," Barbara explained, "which clearly it's not."

"Clearly," Jordi echoed.

"I don't want to worry you," Barbara said, "but you might have to move back to your mothers either way."

"Will she still get the inheritance?" Jordi asked.

Barbara looked at her grand-niece in disappointment, "actually, considering Elizabeth came back into my life because of you, I think no."

"No?" Jordi asked.

"No," Barbara said, "If my house is to be repossessed, your mother will not receive her inheritance."

Jordi went downstairs and called Faith.

"Faith, what is going on?" Jordi asked, into the phone, "okay, see you soon," she flopped on the couch by Michelle's feet.

"Faith will fix this," Jordi said to herself.

"Have you spoken to your mum?" Michelle asked.

Jordi sat up and looked at her, "you're talking. And no," Jordi said, "I don't want her to know anything."

"Why?" Michelle asked.

"She's going to be so disappointed," Jordi said, "she really wanted me to excel at something and I'm not excelling at anything."

"You are being as awesome as you can be and that's something to be proud of," Michelle said "Not all of us can excel to great lengths, but we can be proud of what we can do."

"You're quite right," Jordi said, "I'm constantly feeling like there's more that I could be doing, I just don't know how to do it."

"Same," Michelle agreed, "but we're not all built the same."

"I just wish I could fix everyone's problems. Like Faith does."

"Look at Faith," Michelle said, "she lives with her parents to save her money and doesn't have to think about things like dinner every night, or how long the washing is going to take or where her next rent payment is coming from so she can focus on other things, like helping her friends. Look at me, I'm just focusing on resting and trying to wake up in the morning so I can live my best life in the future, I'm using all my energy just to eat, drink and stop this meltdown you're having. Faith and I love you for being you. And I couldn't and wouldn't be able to do all the things I'm doing without you, Jordi. I mean that."

"Really?" Jordi asked.

"Look at you," Michelle continued, "you are spending every waking hour taking care of your family, you are making sure Barbara gets fed, she stays well, she is out with her friends and enjoying her life to her fullest. All while taking care of yourself, and me. Most people your age struggle with themselves alone but you've taken on the care of someone else too. And I'm damn proud of you."

Jordi looked to Michelle with bulging eyes. Faith sprinted through the door into the sitting room holding a bag of Fish And Chips.

"What's the problem?" Faith asked.

"I think I'm actually okay," Jordi said, "I might actually be able to figure this one out on my own, thanks Fi."

"You can't be serious," Faith said like a growling dog, "I raced over here, right before sitting down to spaghetti bolognese. Spaghetti bolognese. Do you know how delicious my dads spaghetti bolognese is?"

"Oh. Sorry, Fi," Jordi said, leaning back, away from Faith's wrath.

"I got here as fast as I bloody could," Faith continued growling, "I called the Fish And Chip shop and made them make something special. I got you your damn pineapple fritter and a stupid potato fritter. Why would you want a potato fritter when you already have chips? Why Jordi? Why?"

"I don't know, I'm sorry," Jordi cowered.

"Ridiculous," Faith said.

"Thank you for bringing us some dinner," Jordi said. Faith placed the food on the floor in the middle of the room, "Michelle gets first dibs."

Michelle slid off the couch and sat next to the bag of food. She picked up a potato fritter that had a pyramid of salt on it and ate it with the look of a toddler who just discovered chocolate milk.

"Tell me the problem," Faith said.

"Hold up," Jordi ran out of the room and then ran back in with a plate, "I'm going to take some to Barbara. I must look after her and myself. And I'm proud of that."

Faith looked at Jordi as though she was a mouldy flower stem, "get out of here you weirdo."

"Barbara, I brought you dinner," Jordi said, walking into her bedroom.

"Thank you, dear," Barbara said, sitting up in her bed.

"How can someone repossess a house that isn't theirs?" Jordi asked, placing the plate of Fish and Chips on Barbara's lap.

"It's a complicated process and includes a lot of spite," Barbara said.

"But it's not theirs. I thought this house was gifted to you so it's yours," Jordi said.

"There are always loopholes," Barbara said, "usually you get away with a lot when you find those loopholes, but when those loopholes find you... Things are a little different."

"I just don't understand."

"Thank you for dinner, Jordi," Barbara said, "I shall wish to eat this in peace."

Jordi left the room, she closed the door and almost swore she heard the theme song to The Good Life playing.

"Did Barbara say anything else?" Faith asked.

"She talked about loopholes and loopholes finding her but I don't know what that means," Jordi explained.

"The upper class," Faith said, "you all think you're way above everyone else, it's about time for a reality check."

"I'm sorry," Jordi said to Faith, "which class do you think you're in?"

"Just because my parents might be in one class, doesn't mean I'm in it too," Faith said, "I think that it is completely unfair that loopholes exist."

Jordi rolled her eyes.

"Jordi," Michelle said.

"Yes, Michelle," Jordi said, leaning towards her.

"Does Barbara have a mortgage on her house?" Michelle asked.

"I wouldn't know," Jordi said, "I would assume not considering her age."

Jordi thought for a second.

"Oh god, I hope not considering her age," Jordi went deep into her thoughts.

"I'm glad I don't have a house," Faith said, "Imagine having it be taken away."

Jordi looked at Faith as though she was a fish trying to swim across a dining room table.

"Jordi, I think we need to think about this," Faith said in a level tone, "If she doesn't have a mortgage, no one's taking her house, and if she does have a mortgage, god knows how she's paying for it but she could put that money towards a retirement home instead."

"If she's not paying for it, that's probably why it's being taken from her," Jordi said.

"I suppose that is a good point," Faith admitted.

"Where would she live? Would we all live in my mums house? I don't think we'd fit," Jordi thought about that.

"Doesn't your family live at a winery on Waiheke?" Faith asked.

"They own a vineyard but they all live around the island in rather modest accommodation," Jordi explained, "my mum only has two levels in her home and I can't imagine how Barbara would feel going from three stories to only two."

"I think she'll live," Michelle said, eating a greasy, salty chip.

Chapter 16

The next morning the room stank of grease and oil from the Fish And Chip dinner the night before, salt had managed to sprinkle itself onto both couches and the old paper wrapping was flung to the corner of the room.

"Faith?" Jordi asked, sitting up and seeing her friend.

"I took the week off," Faith said as she combed her hair back.

"You did?"

"I did," Faith said, "but I didn't do it for you, I did it for Michelle."

Michelle pushed herself up into a sitting position on the couch, "guys look, I sat myself up."

Jordi and Faith cheered and shouted praises.

"Nice one, Michelle!"

"You did it, Michelle!"

"Thank you," Michelle said, pretending to bow, "should I risk it with a shower?"

"No!" They shouted in unison.

"Sit still," Faith said, gently placing her hands on Michelle's shoulders, "Jordi, what do we need to get done today?"

"Who knows?" Jordi got up and sat on the couch next to Michelle, "I might have to move back in with my mum either way so I guess the chores don't matter anymore."

"They do matter," Faith said, "whether or not Barbara keeps this house, we need to have the place liveable."

"Why?" Jordi asked, "what's the point?"

"The point is so we can enjoy every moment we have in this home," Faith said.

Jordi looked at her all disgruntled, "I suppose we can pick up all the sticks outside and do something with them?"

"We could play a giant game of pick up sticks," Faith suggested.

"Or we could make bivouacs?" Michelle suggested.

"That sounds more fun," Faith said, "you go make a bivouac and I'll find out what's going on with Barbara," Faith said.

Michelle jumped up from the couch with enthusiasm.

"Not you, Michelle," Faith scolded, "you can watch and help with light work only."

"I agree," Jordi said.

Michelle lost all her enthusiasm and sat back on the couch next to Jordi.

"It's okay, Michelle," Jordi said, "you can be the bivouac tester and rate each one I make."

"Alright," Michelle said.

Jordi and Michelle made their way into the garden while Faith took herself upstairs.

Faith gave a soft knock on the bedroom door and called out, "Barbara, it's Faith, can I come in?"

"You may," Barbara said with some confusion.

Faith strolled into the room full of purpose, she pulled the stool out from under the vanity and sat on it facing Barbara who was still in bed.

"We need to talk about your house and how it's being taken from you," Faith stated, "I don't trust Jordi to get any information so I'm doing it myself."

Barbara sat up with her legs over the side of the bed and looked Faith directly in the eyes, "this sounds serious."

"It is serious," Faith said, "fill me in."

"Well," Barbara said, removing herself from the intense eye contact and shuffling her gaze all around the room, "Elizabeth claims I owe her money from the business we used to own, and apparently this house has always been in her name, and apparently she has oh so kindly let me live in it all these years, and I don't have the money to buy it back. Allegedly."

"My god," Faith said.

"Alledgedly," Barbara stated, "but I'll believe it when I see it."

"Geez," Faith sighed, "you live in as much denial as Jordi does."

"Yes, well..." Barbara started and didn't finish.

"So there's nothing we can do?" Faith asked.

"This house is worth three point seven million and-"
"What?" Faith exclaimed in disbelief.
"And I just don't have that kind of money anymore,"
Barbara said.
"And the threats with your sister?" Faith asked, "can't
she give you some money?"
"How do you know about that?" Barbara looked taken
aback.
"Jordi told us."
"Oh, dear," Barbara said, "that girl never could keep
her mouth shut."
"She's my friend."
"That's very good, dear," Barbara said, "but what are
we going to do?"
"Ask your sister for money," Faith stated.
"Oh no, I can't do that," Barbara said.
"Why not?" Faith asked.
"I'll tell you but this is just between you and me,
okay?"
"Okay," Faith nodded.
"She thinks I'm a bit of an imbecile."
"What?" Faith smiled.
"She's always been a bit upset about the way I left the
family and she thinks I'm a tad financially
irresponsible."
"That's. Well. That's a reasonable conclusion."
"No, I don't think so," Barbara said, "she's been put in
charge of all our families finances, self appointed of
course, and won't give me any money unless it's for a
good reason."
"Buying back your house is not a good reason?" Faith
asked.

"No," Barbara said, "she's a bit of a control freak and thinks she knows best. She said she'd buy me a place in the Edmund Hillary Retirement Village but that's just insane, I'm nowhere near that stage in my life, she's absolutely ridiculous and selfish."

"But how would you follow through with your threat to Jordi?" Faith asked.

"You see, my sister has said she can give me some money to keep the house if Jordi stays with me for over a year," Barbara explained, "It's just about been a year and if Jordi stays with me only a couple more weeks, my sister will see Jordi as a dependant and she'll make sure her granddaughter has everything she needs to be taken care of, through me of course."

Faith stood up from her stool and looked down upon Barbara.

"This is just between you and me, of course," Barbara stated again.

"So, Jordi's mum would never get her beach house in the coromandel?" Faith stammered.

"Oh, of course she would," Barbara waved a hand as though she smelt something bad, "I'm sure there's plenty of money to go around."

"Billy T. James," Faith called. A bump in Barbara's blankets rose.

"I think I must go," Faith backed away towards the door. She called Billy T. James who slowly rose at a leisurely pace, he stretched and yawned as he made his way out of Barbara's bed, he then sauntered over to Barbara and curled up on her lap. Faith turned around and left the room.

She ran outside to the garden and watched the
childlike innocence of Jordi building a little hut over top
of Michelle who sat on the broken lawnmower.

"I need a veranda," Michelle called as Jordi raced
around her, "And solar panels."

"Jordi!" Faith called, walking out towards the
construction site.

"Busy," Jordi responded.

"I want a Mai Tai," Michelle said, holding out her hand.

"Jordi!" Faith called again.

"Only employees who have signed in at the gate can
enter the site," Jordi said, "health and safety."

Faith grabbed the top of the bivouac and pushed it to
the ground. Jordi stopped what she was doing and
stared at Faith in disbelief.

"Jordi, we have to leave," Faith said, "all of us, we
can't stay here."

"If I leave, I'm never welcome back," Jordi said.

"I think that's a good thing," Faith said.

"I think that's a bad thing," Jordi said.

"Jordi," Faith said, "can we just have an adult
conversation, please."

"After you knocked down Michelle's hut I was custom
building for her, I don't think so."

"Jordi," Faith said, "this is serious, I was just talking to
Barbara-"

"I know what I'm doing, Faith," Jordi said, "I can look
after myself, just butt out."

Faith raised her eyebrows at Jordi.

"You think I'm not capable of anything but I think
otherwise and you need to give me room to be

myself," Jordi said, standing her ground and piercing her gaze into Faith's.

"I spoke to Barbara and the house is being repossessed," Faith explained.

"We already know this," Jordi said, trying to rebalance the sticks over Michelle.

"I'm not talking to you," Faith said, "Michelle, she said if Jordi stays with her long enough, her sister will give her money to aid in Jordi's care."

"What?" Jordi looked at Faith.

"And if she gets that money, she'll be able to buy her house back," Faith explained.

Jordi thought for a second, "And the money for my mum?"

"Apparently there's plenty to go around," Faith said, "you wouldn't even need to be kissing Barbara's feet, it was all lies."

"Is there any money for me?" Jordi asked.

"You'll have to ask your real grandmother," Faith said, "she's in charge of family accounts."

"Family accounts?" Jordi said, surprised, "that sounds like nonsense."

"That's what Barbara said," Faith stated.

"And she sounded coherent?" Jordi asked.

"Very."

"That's really odd," Jordi said.

"Call your mum and ask her," Michelle suggested.

"But what if it's not true?" Jordi said, "she'll think I'm a wackjob."

"She's your mum," Michelle said, "she probably already believes you're a wackjob."

"But I don't want her to think I'm more of a wackjob than I already am," Jordi said.

"That'll be pretty hard to do," Michelle said.

Jordi and Faith gave Michelle the side eye of the century.

"If you leave," Faith said, "Barbara won't get her money."

"Which is bad," Jordi said.

"No, that's good," Faith said.

"How is it good?" Jordi asked.

"She's manipulating you," Faith said.

"How?" Jordi asked.

"In the way that I just told you," Faith growled.

"But we want her to keep the house," Jordi said.

Faith stopped and thought for a moment, "we want you to be treated with respect."

"But if I leave, what will happen to Barbara?" Jordi asked.

"Your grandma will buy her a place in a retirement home," Faith explained.

"That's nice," Jordi said.

"Jordi-" Faith began.

"How can you buy a place in a retirement home?" Jordi asked, "what happens to it after you die?"

"I think your kids get it," Michelle said.

"So you could buy it like property?" Jordi asked.

"No, I don't think that's right," Faith said, "It would be more like a leasehold so when you pass on, it gets given back to the village"

"But how does that make sense?" Michelle asked, "does that mean retirement villages are just one big scam?"

"Everything is a scam these days," Jordi said, going off to look for more sticks.

"They have to earn money somehow, and they do a lot of good work for the people living there," Faith said.

"I suppose," Michelle shrugged.

"So Jordi, you have to leave and your great-aunt can live her best life in one of those villages," Faith brought them back to the topic at hand.

"Where would I go?" Jordi asked.

"Anywhere," Faith said, "Barbara is using you."

"I'm kind of using her too," Jordi said, creating a veranda of sticks for Michelle's lawn mower house.

"Yes," Faith said, "we are all painfully aware of that but you have to stick up for yourself."

Jordi stopped building the veranda and looked at Faith, "I need her for a place to live. She needs me for financial gain, isn't it a win-win on both sides?"

"You mean, you don't care?" Faith asked, "you don't care that she treats you like dirt on the bottom of her shoe and you don't care that she's not thinking about your welfare or your benefit at all in this situation?"

"We both need a place to live and if staying here means she can keep a roof over her head and mine, then I'm in," Jordi said.

"You don't even need to do all this labour, she's just making you do it for nothing," Faith said.

"It sounds like she doesn't have any money to hire someone else to do it," Jordi shrugged, "I guess I'm kind of, actually, understanding her situation."

"Absolutely ridiculous," Faith said, "Michelle?"

Michelle shrugged, "Jordi's choice, if she wants to carry on living on the tail wind of someone else, that's her choice. When she wants to fly, she'll fly."
Faith stared at Michelle.
"I agree with Michelle," Jordi said, "this is my choice and if I choose to help my grandmother, I can."
"Which grandmother?" Faith asked.
"The fake one, the one upstairs," Jordi explained.
"This is Stockholm Syndrome," Faith said, exasperated.
"You live at home too, Faith," Jordi explained, "you would do the same if your parents were losing their house."
"My parents treat me with respect," Faith stated.
"If all I have to do is stay here and not leave, I can do that," Jordi said.
"She's manipulating you."
"She's old," Jordi said, "And now I know I don't actually have to do anything around the house because she won't kick me out."
Jordi's face suddenly lost all colour and she ran indoors.

Chapter 17

"Barbara!" Jordi called barging into her great-aunts room, "your friend! Your friend! She took the furniture."
"What?" Barbara said, with The Good Life playing on her TV.
"She took all my furniture, I bet she did it," Jordi puffed after her sprint, "she took it as pay back."
"Interesting," Barbara said, "how did you come to this conclusion?"
"If she's going to take the house, why not take the furniture too?"

"Yes, that is a very good idea," Barbara said, "a strong possibility."

"We should search her house," Jordi said.

"And how do you plan on doing that?" Barbara asked, patting Billy T. James.

"We could sneak into her house in the dead of night and look for- Is that a TV?" Jordi asked, looking at where Barbara's painting used to be. Barbara lifted the remote and changed the TV back to a picture by Pierre-Joseph Buc'hoz of a soft pink Hyacinths.

"Don't worry about that," Barbara said, "how would you get away with that kind of illegal activity?"

"We'd be really quiet," Jordi said.

"You are anything but, I'm afraid," Barbara said, "but that is a lovely thought. No, we must go about this in the most legal way possible."

"Can't your other siblings help?" Jordi asked.

"My sister holds all the finances for the family so I'm afraid it's up to her," Barbara explained. "But I'm sure she'll come through for me at the last minute."

"Does she usually?" Jordi asked.

"No," Barbara said, "not this one. Perhaps if I talk to the baby and get her on my side, she could advocate for me."

"That's sweet," Jordi said, "having siblings sounds really nice."

"You are the lucky one," Barbara said, "siblings are a nightmare."

"Really?" Jordi asked, "would you choose to be an only child if you could give away your siblings?"

"Not ever," Barbara stated, "what a nasty thought. No, I couldn't live without my special botherations. No, I would never give them up."

Jordi looked at her great-aunt in confusion, "so what are we going to do?"

"By now I see Faith broke our bond of trust. Go tell your friends I suggest we do nothing and to hope for the best," Barbara said.

"That's all?" Jordi asked.

"That is all we can do for the moment."

"Surely someone knows what to do?" Jordi asked.

"Ask your friend, Faith," Barbara suggested, "she seems to have an answer for everything."

Jordi knitted her eyebrows together, "you're really going to do nothing?"

"As long as you stay under my roof, we just might be lucky," Barbara said before changing her painting back to a TV screen.

Jordi left her great-aunts room and went back outside to be with her friends, making a detour to the kitchen first.

"I brought you all water," Jordi said, handing out glasses of ice cold Fiji water.

"What did Barbara say?" Faith asked.

"She just wants to wait and hope for the best," Jordi said, "And do nothing, she's just watching TV."

"I'm starting to see where you get it from," Faith said, taking a sip of water, "It sounds like you both handle stress in the same way."

"I don't sit around watching TV," Jordi protested.

"That's exactly what you did," Faith retorted.

"When?" Jordi asked, "I think I've handled this stress pretty well."

"What are we going to do now?" Faith asked.

"I think Elizabeth is the one who broke into the house and took all my things," Jordi explained.

"Why would she do that?" Faith asked.

"If she's going to take the house, why not take the furniture too?" Jordi said.

"But if she's already going to take the house, why would she need to take the furniture early?" Faith asked.

"Wouldn't you? A game of power to scare away the enemy."

"Jordi," Faith said, "you're sounding ridiculous."

"Are you saying my reaction is not perfectly reasonable?" Jordi asked like an insecure sibling who's not getting enough attention.

"I can't deal with you," Faith said, turning to Michelle, "how are you? Is your energy still feeling stable?"

"I'm a tad bored just sitting," Michelle said, "Faith, do you remember when you were my PT?"

"Yeah, that's how we met," Faith said, "you were a good client, you pushed yourself to breaking point. Kind of literally."

"Yeah. You broke me," Michelle said, "that one session after Covid is how I've become a life long invalid."

"Don't say that," Faith snapped, "your circumstances might change, you never know."

"Maybe," Michelle shrugged, "but what if it is lifelong?"

"Then so be it," Faith said, "we'll build you a million bivouacs and create a reality tv show about young people with long covid living in bivouacs. The only homes they'll ever afford"

Michelle laughed.

"Maybe you'll even write your own show," Faith suggested.

"Maybe," Michelle shrugged.

"Or a cookbook," Faith said.

"Soooooo," Jordi chimed in, "you guys want to steal back my things from Barbara's not-friend?"

"I suppose if she took them," Faith said, "do you know where they'll be?"

"No idea," Jordi said.

"I'll help," Michelle volunteered with the energy of a seven year old on Christmas morning.

Jordi looked her up and down, "you will be able to fit through all the tight spaces. Faith, you're our muscle, I'll be the brains."

"You'll be the brains?" Faith asked with distaste.

"You can go home if you're not happy here," Jordi stated to Faith.

"Why?" Faith asked, "so you can call me on the phone crying again?"

"That never happened," Jordi said.

"I was there," Faith said, "And I'll be your lookout."

Chapter 18

Jordi served chicken-less chicken nuggets and
steamed frozen vegetables to Barbara for dinner.
"You can't complain," Jordi said, "I know you won't
kick me out."
Barbara took the plate and sighed as she continued
watching The Good Place, no longer hiding her secret
TV.

"Yes, I guess that might be true," Barbara said, "It is a shame, you were doing so well here, I almost recommended you for a job."

"You did?" Jordi asked.

"Almost," Barbara corrected.

Jordi's face fell and she left the room feeling as though Barbara had just stamped all over her.

Night fell and Jordi and Faith were dressed in black, tight clothing. Michelle refused to do any unnecessary physical activity so she could join in with the evening escapades. She wore sweat-pants and a t-shirt.

"Faith and I know which house it is," Jordi explained, "from there, we'll work as a team to find the furniture and bring as much as we can back to Barbara's."

"You want to bring it back?" Faith asked, "you don't just want to take photos and send them to the Police?"

"And let them know we broke into someone's property?" Jordi asked, "no. This is personal."

"And I'm staying outside," Faith stated.

"Correct," Jordi said, bouncing from one foot to the other.

"And what do I do if I see something suspicious?" Faith asked.

"Call us," Jordi said, "or text us."

Faith nodded, "alright. And I can run off, right?"

"Yeah," Jordi said, "get away as fast as you can but make sure you text us."

"Alright, I can do that," Faith said, "And what counts as something suspicious?"

"Use your judgement," Jordi said.

"But what if I think it's suspicious and it's not suspicious?" Faith asked.

"Better safe than sorry," Jordi said, jiggling her knees and sliding her fingers along the tip of her thumb.

"But what if something happens to me and I can't contact you?" Faith said, the pitch of her voice getting higher and higher.

"No one's dying," Jordi reassured.

"You don't know that," Faith almost screeched. Her breathing sped up and she sat down hugging her knees. Jordi knelt down next to her.

"Faith, if you don't want to do this you don't have to." Faith looked at Jordi with a mix of relief and guilt.

"We can carry on and you can stay back and make sure the beds are ready for us to act as though we've been asleep all night. You can make sure we all have a cup of tea ready and waiting for when we get back. Maybe, you could play some music so it sounds like we're at home throwing a party."

Faith nodded, "I can do that."

"I'll make you a cup of tea," Jordi said. She came back and handed Faith the warm mug. She looked at Michelle, "should we go?"

She nodded. Michelle clung onto Jordi's arm and they made their way to the gate where the gruff sounding woman had insulted Barbara through her gate phone.

"This is it," Jordi said.

"Michelle, you think you can climb over this?" Jordi asked.

Michelle nodded.

"I'll give you a leg up," Jordi said, linking her hands together for Michelle to put her foot into. Michelle

leaned against the gate as Jordi lifted her until her arms were over the top of the gate. She swung her leg over and sat on the top looking out towards the ocean. Jordi gave a little jump, "I'm stuck," Jordi said, hanging and gripping the gate with both hands in a panic.
"You got this, Jordi," Michelle said, in a loud whisper. Jordi managed to pull herself up with all her might and all the adrenaline that rushed through her body.
"Let's go," Michelle said, holding the gate and swinging her legs over to the side of the driveway. She let go and hit the ground with bent legs, she let herself crumble and roll, jumping back up on two feet.
"This is the best night of my life," Michelle said, throwing her arms into the air.
Jordi tried to follow in Michelle's footsteps. She gripped onto the gate and maneuvered her legs until they were both hanging off the side of the driveway. Jordi lost her grip and fell towards the ground. She crumbled and rolled, laying on the ground looking up at the stars.
"You okay?" Michelle asked, standing over Jordi looking down at her red face.
"Ground shock," Jordi said.
"Stay lying down," Michelle advised, "we can wait." They waited only moments until Jordi was ready and Michelle helped her up from the ground.
"Did you see that?" Michelle asked.
"See what?" Jordi looked all around her.
"I helped you up," Michelle said in an excited whisper, "I. Helped. You," Michelle squealed with delight and skipped down the driveway.
"Wait," Jordi tried to shout in a whisper.

"Sorry," Michelle said.

They walked together down the winding driveway past a tree lined path and rose bushes. Garden lights helped guide the way towards the house.

"How long is this driveway?" Jordi asked.

They went around a sharp corner and were met with a four story home, all black except for golden lights shining from the windows.

"We should have watched the house to figure out her routine so we came on a night she was out," Michelle said.

"It's too late now," Jordi charged on.

"Wait," Michelle whispered, "are we just knocking on the door?"

Jordi stopped, "we can climb through a window without a light on."

"How do we get in?" Michelle asked.

"You're thin," Jordi said, "you could squeeze through."

Michelle raised an eyebrow. They could hear some music coming from next door. Jordi and Michelle both smiled.

They walked up to the side of the house and saw one window perched open.

"I think you could fit," Jordi said, looking at Michelle.

"You think?" Michelle asked.

Jordi looked at her in the dark, they hadn't brought torches with them but Jordi could just make out Michelle's face with the light from a window above.

"Are you okay to jump or do you want me to give you a leg up?" Jordi asked.

Michelle's face lit up, "I'll jump."

She turned around and placed her finger tips on the window sill. She assessed the gap and decided she could fit her head through but only just. She placed one foot up against the wall and with the other, she leaped, ran up the wall, threw her arms inside the window, and pulled herself through like a slippery snake. She landed with her hands leaning on a closed toilet lid and her legs in the air. She lowered herself down and let herself fall on her side on the floor.

"Jordi, can you make it?" Michelle whispered through the window.

"Not through this window," Jordi whispered back, "we'll need to find another entrance."

"Alright."

"You okay?" Jordi asked.

"Yeah."

"You sure?"

"Yeah."

Michelle rubbed her arms and could already see some bruises forming. Her head felt like her brain had swelled and was pushing against the inside of her skull. Her right wrist felt like she twisted it and when she lifted up her shirt she could see a large bruise around her lower ribs already formed in angry purple.

"I'll meet you at the front door," Michelle whispered.

"That seems a bit risky," Jordi said.

"We're here for risk, are we not?" Michelle said with her enthusiasm dialed all the way down. Her head felt heavy and her thoughts were foggy. She was in a bathroom and she needed to let Jordi in. She lent over and tried to push the window open but it wouldn't budge.

"Jordi," Michelle whispered, "Jordi, you won't make it through the window," she looked down but Jordi was no longer outside. She felt around the room until her finger tips felt a light switch, she clicked it. The light shone hurting her eyes as though someone had flicked a rubber band towards them. She turned the lights off and felt her way towards the door, she turned the door handle and entered into a bedroom. She could see a bedside lamp was on but apart from that, the room looked untouched. There was a Super King size bed in the middle, two bedside tables; one with a lamp that was on and one with a seashell. Across from the bed was a chest of drawers and a full length mirror. Michelle instinctively went over to the lamp and turned it off to save electricity. She then walked out of the bedroom and made her way to the entrance of the house. She walked on tiled floor coloured in black and white to the entrance, next to the doorway was a side table only big enough for one vase of flowers. Michelle bent down and felt the tile, these were cool on her hand and they calmed her nervous system. She brought her hands back up to her forehead, momentarily soothing her skull.

She heard footsteps coming towards her, jolting her into an upright position. She ran towards the door, pulled it open and flung herself outside, bumping right into Jordi as the door slammed behind her.

"Are you okay?" Jordi asked.

"Someone was coming," Michelle said.

"Okay," Jordi nodded, "you did the right thing, tell me what you saw-"

The front door opened and Elizabeth stood in the entrance way.

"Can I help you?" She asked.

Michelle stood paralyzed.

"We just came over to see if we could borrow some sugar," Jordi said, "I'm baking a cake."

"You want some sugar?" Elizabeth asked.

"Yes," Jordi said.

"What happened to your eye?" Elizabeth pointed to Michelle's face. Jordi looked and saw a newly formed bruise on the side of Michelle's face that creeped around her right eye.

"You have a bruise," Jordi said, pointing.

"Oh, it's nothing," Michelle said, "I bruise easy. I probably walked into a tree or something."

"Or something, I suspect," Elizabeth said, "come in and I'll get some ice for you."

"Oh no, you don't have to," Jordi stammered.

Elizabeth looked down at the two of them like a mother who just caught her child trying to relocate a dislocated bone, "get inside and let your sister put ice on her eye."

Jordi and Michelle looked taken aback.

Elizabeth held the door open until the two women had entered her home.

"Last time I saw you," Elizabeth said, leading them into the kitchen, "you were in a wheelchair. Did you just learn how to walk again?"

"No," Michelle answered shortly.

"No?" Elizabeth asked, "that wasn't you learning to walk in my house?"

"What?" Michelle asked.

"You weren't the one snaking through my bathroom window and saving my electricity bill in the bedroom? Bumping into everything it sounded like," Elizabeth looked at her knowingly but she didn't look angry. She wrapped up a frozen sausage roll in a tea towel and handed it to Michelle who held it against her eye.

"Sorry," Michelle whispered.

"Have a seat," Elizabeth gestured to a table and chairs in her kitchen, "the joys of having security cameras," she giggled.

Michelle sat down and pulled her knees up to her chest, looking glum. Jordi took a seat next to her.

"Can you tell me why you were breaking into my house at such an odd hour?" Elizabeth asked. "You'd think people as young as you could at least wait until after midnight."

"We want our furniture back," Jordi said, surprising herself with her confidence.

"Your what?" Elizabeth asked.

"I want my pool table, my tv, my couch and all my things," Jordi said.

"How strange," Elizabeth sat opposite them at the table, passing Michelle and Jordi each a small tub of Lewis Rd Creamery Ice cream and spoons.

"What's this?" Jordi asked.

"You've had a big night," Elizabeth said, "you might need some ice cream."

Jordi popped the lid and saw the chocolatey goodness inside, she scraped a bit off the top and let the creamy sweet nectar melt on her tongue.

"Now that I've buttered you up, can you explain to me about this furniture?" Elizabeth asked.

"We know you are trying to take Barbara's house and we know you took all my things," Jordi stated.

"Part of that is true, I will admit," Elizabeth said, "your grandma owes me a lot and she needs to pay back what she owes."

"But you have this house, you have everything," Jordi said, "why do you need more?"

"I rent the bottom floor of this house to be close to Barbara while she acts like a child," Elizabeth explained, "I've been talking to her family and we've come to an agreement. Your grandma is a slippery creature- is she alright?" Elizabeth gestured to Michelle who had her arms wrapped around her legs and her head leaning forward with the frozen sausage roll on her knees.

"Michelle?" Jordi asked, "are you alright?"

Michelle didn't answer.

"Michelle?" Jordi gave Michelle a nudge. Her head bobbled and the frozen sausage roll fell to the floor but Michelle didn't react, "Michelle?" Jordi's voice became high pitched and she nudged Michelle harder.

Elizabeth moved around the table and stood between Michelle and Jordi, pushing Jordi off and blocking her. With both hands Elizabeth gently moved Michelle's head to an upright position. Michelle's eyes were closed and the edges of her lips blue.

"I'm calling an ambulance."

Chapter 19

Elizabeth, Barbara, Jordi, Faith, and Maggie sat
around Michelle's bed in the emergency department of
Auckland Hospital. Michelle was fast asleep with a
striped gown wrapped around her and an oxygen
mask strapped to her face. Maggie sat next to her
holding her hand.

"What happened?" Maggie asked with a weak voice,
looking at the bruise on Michelle's face.

Nobody answered.

"Jordi, what happened?" Maggie asked again.

"They came to my house to borrow a bit of sugar for some baking," Elizabeth said, "I'm afraid I opened the front door a little too fast and it knocked your daughter right over."

Jordi looked to Elizabeth with gratitude. Barbara looked at Elizabeth with disgust.

"My poor baby," Maggie said, "you were baking?"

"We were going to bake a cake," Jordi said.

"What for?" Maggie asked.

A silence fell over the room.

"It was Billy T. James' birthday," Faith said.

"How lovely," Maggie said, looking at her daughter lying asleep in a hospital bed, "she used to bake for us every birthday," Maggie let out a couple sobs.

"I remember," Jordi said.

"Do you remember that three tier cake she made for your twenty-first, Jordi?" Maggie asked.

"I do," Jordi nodded, "It was dripping with caramel."

"It was dripping with caramel," Maggie laughed through tears, "she needed a ladder to decorate that... She wouldn't be able to climb any ladders now."

"Maybe one day," Faith said, "maybe she'll climb a ladder again."

"No," Maggie shook her head, "no, I don't think she will."

The room was quiet as Maggie squeezed her child's hand.

"She wanted to work on cruise ships and travel the world," Maggie went on, "she wanted to see all the sites and taste all the different spices in every country on the globe."

Everybody listened in respectful silence.

"She was a decent soccer player too," Maggie continued, "And she loved to dance."

A nurse came in and explained they would be moving Michelle to a ward.

"Please go," Maggie said to the others, "I'll stay here for a bit and then I'll go get some rest at home."

"I can stay too," Jordi offered.

"No," Maggie blatantly refused, "I want to be alone with her."

"I'm really sorry, Maggie," Jordi said.

"You were supposed to take care of her," Maggie said, avoiding eye contact with Jordi.

"We were just baking," Jordi lied.

Maggie shook her head, "I know she's young and she wants to have fun when she can, but she's just not capable of that anymore. She can't be treated like a twenty two year old, Jordi. I thought you would know this, I trusted you."

"I'm sorry," Jordi said again.

Maggie followed the nurse pushing her daughter's bed towards a ward. Jordi stood back and watched them go.

Michelle, her nurse and her mum turned down the hospital corridor where Jordi could no longer see them. Jordi turned and joined the others waiting for her outside the emergency department entrance.

"It wasn't your fault," Faith said, wrapping her arm around her friend's waist.

"How can you say that?" Jordi asked, "It was my idea and I pushed her to go through that window."

"She has a disease and it's her responsibility to work with it," Faith said, "all we can do is be there for her."

"I wasn't there for her," Jordi said, "I shouldn't have let her go."

"Do you remember how happy she was to be included? To finally be able to be part of something again?" Faith said, "that brought her a lot of joy."

"At what cost," Jordi said, hanging her head low.

"Let's go home and have some hot chocolate," Faith said.

"Why don't we order some?" Barbara suggested, "I know you love your deliveries, Jordi."

Jordi nodded.

They all went back to Barbara's place in her Tesla, Jordi placed an order for four large hot chocolates to be delivered.

"I didn't realise things could turn so quickly for her," Barbara said, staring at the mess in her sitting room, "or that we didn't have a guest room."

"You have a guest room?" Faith asked.

"It's okay, Barbs," Elizabeth said, spreading her toes amongst the fluffy carpet.

Jordi stayed by the door and collected the delivery.

"Thank you," Elizabeth said, as Jordi handed her her drink.

"Thank you for taking the fall for us," Jordi said, "you really didn't have to do that."

"What's wrong with the poor girl?" Elizabeth asked.

"Been this way since Covid," Faith said.

"Ah yes," Elizabeth nodded, "she's not the only one."

They all sat around drinking their hot chocolates and contemplating the events from the late night.

"Tell me about this furniture you've accused me of stealing," Elizabeth asked.

Barbara went bright red, "sorry?"

"Your grandchildren broke into my home accusing me of taking your furniture," Elizabeth explained, "and they clearly know one side of the story when it comes to this house."

"Yes," Barbara nodded, "my grandchildren are very protective of me, they love me very much."

Elizabeth looked at Barbara with a questioning gaze.

"Did you really break into her house?" Barbara asked Jordi.

"We did," Jordi nodded.

Barbara let a small smile creep into her features.

"I did not take your furniture," Elizabeth said.

An awkward silence fell over the room. The moonlight poured into the lounge and the stars sparkled in the night sky outside the sitting room windows.

"Please don't take our house," Jordi said, behind her big cup of hot chocolate.

"You're very lucky to live in such a beautiful home," Elizabeth said, "what's your favourite hobby at the moment?"

"I was really into this online game but I can't play it anymore."

"You had fun building bivouacs," Faith said, with sleepless bloodshot eyes.

"I did," Jordi nodded, her eyes matching Faith's.

"Are you working?" Elizabeth asked.

"Don't tell her anything," Barbara demanded.

"Barbs," Elizabeth sighed, "It's been quite the night, let's just forget it for the moment."

"Never," Barbara said, "but we could watch a movie, I don't mind if you all want to sit on my carpet in my bedroom. Just for tonight."

They all brought their hot chocolates into Barbara's bedroom and sat around watching her TV that spent most of its days disguised as a picture frame. Billy T. James strolled over to Faith and curled up in her lap.

Chapter 20

Jordi received a text from Maggie saying Michelle was awake and ready to receive visitors. The sun was burning hot in the middle of the sky and Jordi and Faith sprinted to Barbara's Tesla and drove as fast as the traffic lights would allow.

The two of them hugged Maggie and stood around Michelle's bed.

"I'm sorry Michelle," Jordi said.

"Don't be," Michelle whispered. She had an oxygen tube up her nose and wires coming out of her veins.

"She can come home today," Maggie said, bags under her eyes and tear stains noticeable on her cheeks.

"That's good news," Faith said, squeezing Maggie's hand.

"But no more climbing gates and squeezing through windows," Maggie informed them with nothing but love in her voice.

"I had to tell the doctor," Michelle whispered, "too many bruises for baking."

"I shouldn't have let you go," Jordi said, "I'm really, truly sorry, Michelle."

Michelle shook her head, "It was… I had… There was a great time."

"Still got a bit of brain fog, don't you sweetie?" Maggie cooed.

Michelle nodded.

"She'll need a lot of rest after this one," Maggie said, "we won't push her for a while but anytime any of you girls want to visit, you're more than welcome."

"Really?" Jordi asked, "You're not mad?"

"I was last night, Jordi. You must understand the shock of it all," Maggie said, looking towards a sad and regretful Jordi, "but you gave my daughter a night she will remember for the rest of her life, I'm sure, and she doesn't get a lot of opportunity to have a night like that. So. No, I am not mad."

Jordi gave Maggie a hug.

"But I don't want to get another call saying my daughter has been ambulanced to hospital after breaking and entering into a house ever again, do you hear me?"

Jordi let out a laugh of relief, "I hear you. Never again."

"And if you need a place to stay," Maggie said, "the option is still there, but I will require you to inform me of every location you are taking my daughter."

"Thank you, Maggie," Jordi said.

"Same goes for you," Maggie said, looking at Faith, "If you need a place to stay, you are most welcome."

"Thanks, Maggie," Faith said, "that's really kind."

Maggie turned back to Michelle with the purple and blue bruise on half her face, "this could've happened anywhere, and knowing my daughter this could've easily happened when she was on her own. I'm just glad you were all with her."

"Jordi was with her," Faith corrected.

"I'm glad you were all there for her," Maggie said.

The doctor came around and discharged Michelle. Faith helped her walk to Maggie's car.

"Do you need a lift?" Maggie asked. Faith and Jordi shook their heads.

"No," Faith said, "but thank you for your kind offer, we'll come visit soon."

The two of them drove the Tesla back to Barbara's.

"Now what?" Faith asked.

"Now we stop Elizabeth from taking our house," Jordi answered.

"She said she didn't take the furniture," Faith said, "And the house is legally hers."

"I don't believe her for a second, she must have some storage unit back there," Jordi said.

"This is going a little far, Jordi. Look what happened to Michelle," Faith said.

"It wasn't me that did that to her, it was Elizabeth who's trying to ruin our lives."

"Jordi, let's be real here," Faith said, "Barbara said the name of the home owner is Elizabeth, she let Barbara stay here out of the goodness of her heart, and now it's time to return the favour."

"But why now?"

"I imagine she just had enough," Faith said, "or she was finally able to kick Barbara out."

"I still hate her."

"Do you, Jordi?" Faith asked, "this woman helped you and Michelle while you were breaking into her home. She made sure you were both fed and safe. She took care of you and she even took care of Barbara. Be honest with yourself. You can't hate someone who has helped so many people."

"Yes, I can."

"Where would Michelle be if Elizabeth was a different person?" Faith asked, "not many people would make sure their intruder was safely in an ambulance."

"Not many people would go breaking and entering."

"No," Faith stated, "they wouldn't, but you did."

Jordi sighed, "I'll see what Barbara's up to," she headed up the stairs and knocked on the door.

"Come in," Barbara said.

Jordi came in and saw Barbara sitting at her vanity.

"How are you?" Jordi asked.

"I'm okay," Barbara said, "still taking in all the events from the past week. And how about yourself, are you handling things okay?"

Jordi nodded, "we saw Michelle in the hospital, she's been sent home."

"That was quick," Barbara looked astonished.

"Is Elizabeth still trying to take this house from you?" Jordi asked.

"Nothing has changed in that department," Barbara said, "I'm afraid one movie won't fix a lifetime of what she believes to be an injustice."

"Why now?" Jordi asked.

"Lizzie always wanted to retire in this home," Barbara smiled to herself, "but I wish I could stay just as much as she does."

"How's it going with your sister?"

"Ah yes," Barbara said, "thank you for reminding me, I must call the baby today and she'll talk to that feline of a sister for me."

"Good luck."

"Thank you, Jordan," Barbara nodded at her. Jordi went back downstairs and sat on the couch.

"It feels weird without Michelle," Jordi noted.

"She's recovering at home, that's the best thing for her," Faith said.

"I just miss her," Jordi said.

"I bet you do," Faith said, folding up the sheets, "how long have you known her?"

"Met in kindy," Jordi explained, "Mum would ride with me on the ferry and go to business classes while I played."

"That's a long time to know a person," Faith noted.

"She used to be the life of the party," Jordi commented.

"And a real fitness freak," Faith said.

"That she was," Jordi agreed.

"I remember when I made you two do my classes together. Do you remember that, Jordi?" Faith asked.

"Yeah, I wasn't so fond of those," Jordi laughed.

"And then we'd all go out for brunch after," Faith reminisced, "she'd always get so enthusiastic over the green smoothies, she wanted to taste one from every place to find the absolute best."

"Did she ever find the best of the best?" Jordi asked.

Faith shook her head, "not that I remember. None could beat her homemade green power smoothie."

"I never tried that," Jordi said, "was it good?"

"If you like kale and peanut butter, which she does," Faith remarked.

"She also added blueberries and honey, right?" Jordi remembered, "I remember her telling me about her recipe. We should make that for her."

"Yeah, we should," Faith agreed.

Jordi's phone buzzed in her pocket. She lifted it up and saw the caller ID read: MUM.

"Mum?" She answered.

"Baby, how are you?"

"Mum, everything's gone wrong."

"I heard, sweetie. How's Michelle?"

"She's okay, she's with her mum who's looking after her."

"That's good. And how are you?"

"I just feel like I've failed everybody."

"You could never fail me, darling. Tell me, how do you think you failed everybody?"

"Michelle's sick because of me, Faith's mad at me because I'm siding with Barbara, and I can't live up to Barbara's expectations," Jordi pouted.

"Hun, it sounds like you've been having a hard time. Did you want to come here and stay for a couple days? Let Barbara organise herself with the move?"

"You know about that?"

"Of course," Jordi's mum said, "It's been in the works for months, I think we've had her room at the retirement village on hold for almost a year now."

"A year?" Jordi asked.

"Of course," her mum said, "I thought you knew this, you moved in to take care of her while we waited for the room to be available. We have a friend of hers who actually owns the home taking it back and handling all the property details."

"I had no idea," Jordi said, "I thought I was here as punishment for ruining her business."

"Oh, baby," her mum coo'd, "Barbara's never been a good business woman, and honestly, she's a hard woman to be around so we do appreciate everything you've done. Did you want to come back here for a couple nights?"

"Honestly, I think I need to hang around here for a bit," Jordi said, "I want to be near Michelle in case she or

Maggie needs me. And this is a lot to process, it might be best if I just have my own space for a bit."

"You sure, hun?"

"I'm sure, thank you though," Jordi said, "love you, bye."

Jordi hung up the phone and placed it down beside her.

"I heard," Faith said, putting her arms around Jordi's shoulders, "I'm not mad at you, Jordi. You've got a lot to process."

"This was the plan all along," Jordi shuddered, "everyone knew about it except me."

"Do you think Barbara was aware?"

"No idea," Jordi stared at the wall, letting the information sink in. Her world felt like a tornado surrounding her with debris flying everywhere. Every person in her life had told her a different story and she didn't know who's side she was on or who she could trust.

"Could I stay with you for a bit?" Jordi asked.

"Of course," Faith agreed, "do you want to talk about it?"

"Why? Just why?" Jordi asked, "why was I made to believe I was the problem, I was the one causing all the issues. Why was I made out to be the bad guy when everything was a plan all along. All of it."

"Jordi, I'm sorry you felt that way."

"Everyone told me I was doing something wrong and needed to step up my game, do better, be better, yet all those people who were telling me that are lying, cheating-"

"That's enough," Faith said.

"Even my own mother made me believe this was all my fault and a punishment for something she now claims I didn't really do."

"Jordi," Faith said, "that's really hard, I'm really sorry."

"It's okay," Jordi said, "honestly, I've survived this long. I can keep going."

Faith lay back in the sitting room, "you can keep going. And you will."

"Oh my god," Jordi slapped her forehead, "I keep forgetting to unload the dishwasher."

"Leave it," Faith said, "the evil lady taking this house can do it."

"I don't think she's evil anymore," Jordi said, "It was lucky she found us when she did. But I appreciate you taking my side."

"Let's take Michelle this dress I got her and see if Maggie needs anything," Faith said.

Jordi picked up a shopping bag with a light, cotton black dress, Faith followed her out the door. They took the Tesla and drove to Michelle's house. They knocked on the door but there was no answer. They knocked again.

Light footsteps were heard and the lock in the door turned. The door cracked open two centimetres.

"I'm not ready for visitors," Maggie said through the door.

"Maggie, it's us," Jordi said.

"Oh yes," Maggie sighed as she opened the door wide. Her bright smile she often wore was nowhere to be seen.

Jordi stepped in first, turned sideways and shuffled down the hallway no longer filled with banana boxes.

The wall was filled with photos from Michelle's time growing up. There was a picture of her as a seven year old on a soccer team, grabbing a piece of orange along with her six team mates; there was a photo of her as a twelve year old in a ballet uniform; as a teenager she was diving from a diving board at the pools with a group of friends. Jordi kept walking towards the open plan kitchen, dining and lounge. She looked out into the overgrown garden. Faith followed.

"Can we do anything for you?" Faith asked.

Maggie shook her head, "no, but thank you so much for your kindness."

"We can bring you some lunch," Faith said.

"No," Maggie shook her head again.

"We bought a dress for Michelle," Jordi held up her bag.

"Thank you, you can take it into her room and hang it up," Maggie said, opening the door to Michelle's room. Michelle was asleep in her bed. Her eyelids didn't even flutter as everyone walked in. There were no piles of clothes on the floor, no mess.

Michelle's bed was now on the other side of the room with the headboard pressed up against the windows with the curtains open and the sun rays hitting Michelle's exposed face.

"Sunlight is good for her," Maggie said.

"It is," Faith nodded.

"Her desk is gone," Jordi commented.

"I did a little rearranging," Maggie let out a small laugh, "her room got a good clean while she was staying with you."

"Do you need someone to stay?" Faith asked, "help you care for her?"

Maggie shook her head, "It's a mother's job."

"You don't have to do this alone," Faith said.

"I've done it alone up to this point, I can continue on," Maggie said,"she's not a burden."

"Of course she's not," Faith said, "she's anything but."

"We can pop in and help you where we can," Jordi said.

"She's not a burden," Maggie repeated, "I can do this on my own, it's no trouble."

"She doesn't have to be a burden," Faith said, picking up and holding Maggie's hand, "we can still help you."

"Oh, no, dear," Maggie said without a glint of hope in her eyes, "you are children, you sit and I'll feed you, what would you like to eat? Are you hungry?"

"We're okay," Faith said.

"Oh," Maggie's face fell and disappointment wore her like a new layer of skin.

"Actually, I could use a bite to eat," Jordi said, exiting the room and sitting down on a kitchen island stool, forgetting about the bag with the dress on Michelle's bedroom floor.

"So could I," Faith said, also taking a seat.

Maggie's face lit up and a little bit of joy shone through her eyes.

"I'll make us some biscuits and maybe a bean salad for health," Maggie said, "right Jordi? You're still on the bean diet?"

"Still on the beans," Jordi nodded.

Maggie raced around the kitchen grabbing a bowl here and a wooden spoon there, she threw in a can of beans, ripped a bunch of lettuce and threw in a jar of mustard vinaigrette.

"Cookies!" Maggie shouted as though she was declaring a try at a rugby game. She grabbed flour, sending particles of white all over her living space, she poured in milk and choc chips. She grabbed a cucumber from her fridge and chopped it up, throwing it into her salad.

"Eat, eat," Maggie said, laying out three plates on the bench.

Faith walked over and tentatively placed some salad onto her plate.

"Thank you," Faith said.

"You need forks," Maggie grabbed some forks from inside one of her drawers and slid them across the bench.

Faith took a bite of ripped lettuce. Jordi followed suit. Maggie opened three bags of chocolate chips and poured them into the cookie dough mixture.

"You can never have too much chocolate," she said. She spooned the dough onto an oven tray while Jordi and Faith politely ate their bean salad.

"Maggie, I'm sorry, I forgot to put away Michelle's dress," Jordi said, "we bought a new dress for her and I just left it on her floor."

"Go now, she won't mind," Maggie said as she continued scooping the cookie dough onto the oven tray.

Jordi slipped off the stool and into Michelle's room.

"The oven!" Jordi heard Maggie shout. Jordi turned around and saw Maggie turn the oven to two hundred degrees while Faith sat there nervously.

Jordi went into Michelle's room and shut the door behind her.

"We bought you a dress," Jordi said. She walked over to the side of the bed and looked at her friend's face. Only twenty two and she looked worn, her face looked sunken and was just about the same colour pale as her cream white bed linen. The purple and blue bruise shone on the right side of her face, covering her eye. Jordi knew how easily Michelle could bruise, even without her feeling any pain, but she had never seen her get this bad or this beaten from one of their silly escapades.

"I'm so sorry," Jordi whispered, "I'm just going to hang up your dress."

She walked over to the cupboard, opening the door with slow precision, trying not to creak the hinges too loud. Already hanging up were a sea of black, cotton dresses. They all were without buttons and without zips. All light and soft staring at Jordi in the face. She didn't even remove the dress she had brought from it's bag, she just placed the bag at the bottom of the cupboard and let the long dresses cover it.

Michelle's eyes fluttered open, she looked over to Jordi feeling like her neck was a door knob in desperate need of oil. The pain in her body felt like an unimaginable weight, every breath took time and concentration. She saw Jordi moving around near her but she moved so fast, Michelle's brain felt dizzy just from watching. She didn't know what Jordi was doing and she felt no emotion with her in the room. Emotions took too much energy. She closed her eyes and felt the world soften around her, the dizziness stopped as the dark world engulfed Michelle into the peace of stillness. The only energy Michelle needed to expel was to take in her breaths, all she had the energy for. She could hear the cupboard closing, the sound like chalk scraping against her brain, taking away her energy to let her breath out. Her head pounded as she heard a sharp click. The blankets suddenly made her feel like she had an apartment building sitting on top of her chest.

'In and out' she concentrated on slow deep breathing. In and out, that's all she needed to do.

Jordi took another look at her friend before closing the door and crept out of the room, back into the commotion.

"Jordi, can you wait until the cookies are baked?" Maggie asked.

"Of course we can."

"Thank goodness," Maggie sighed in relief, "I forgot to heat up the oven but do you want to play cards?"

Jordi nodded and Maggie pulled out a pack from what looked like thin air. They sat around the table playing Hearts until the oven timer went off.

"Time to eat the cookies." Maggie said, jumping up.

They played cards, shouted and laughed until all the biscuits had been eaten.

"I think we had better go," Faith said, shuffling the deck and placing it on the table in front of Maggie.

"Oh, you're only saying that because you lost," Maggie teased.

"We had better go," Jordi agreed, "but thank you again for everything, Maggie."

"Of course," Maggie said, "not a problem, never a problem, come again."

Jordi parked the Tesla next to an empty moving truck. The back doors were wide open and the emptiness was the size of Barbara's sitting room. Jordi opened the door for Faith.
"What's going on?" Jordi asked as two women dressed in the same black shirt emerged from the basement. They smiled but did not respond as they closed the truck's doors and drove away.
Jordi, followed by Faith, walked through the door into the basement.
"What on earth?" Jordi said as she looked around the fully furnished basement. The carpet was clean without any specs of plaster or wallpaper littering the ground. The 85 inch TV was back on the wall exactly where it had been previously. The couch with the permanent dent on the left most cushion sat there as though it had never moved. And the pool table Jordi had never used sat there like a looming shadow wiping away the past.
"Did I miss something?" Jordi asked.
"Barbara must have gotten the stuff back," Faith said.
"Maybe she's not so bad, after all," Jordi said.
Faith took it all in and looked around.
"Nothing's changed," Jordi noted.
Jordi walked around the room and looked at the tv and ran her hand over the permanent dent on the left most cushion.
"I feel like this isn't real," Jordi commented.
"What do you want to do?" Faith asked.

Jordi looked around and looked at her friend, "let's find Barbara."

They both jogged up the stairs and burst into Barbara's room. She was sitting up on her bed, looking out the window.

"Barbara," Jordi said, "what is going on downstairs?"

"You tell me," Barbara said, "what is going on downstairs?"

"The basement has been refurnished," Jordi stated.

"Refurnished?" Barbara asked, "with what?"

"Well…" Jordi thought.

"Everything is exactly the same as it was," Faith said, "exactly the same. How did you pull it off?"

Barbara looked at them and smiled, "how did I pull *what* off?"

"How did you get the things back from Elizabeth?" Faith asked.

Barbara chuckled.

"I believe, Jordan, although you have not learnt the lesson I wished for you too, you have done enough to deserve your little woman cave back."

"What do you mean?" Jordi asked.

"I figured with the house leaving my possession in only three days time, I thought you could enjoy the house for these last moments," Barbara said.

"I don't understand," Jordi stated.

"Oh, Jordan," Barbara looked at Jordi with annoyance, "I thought you would like to have your things, do you not?"

"Did you take them?" Jordi asked.

"Jordan."

"Did you take them?" Jordi growled.

"Jordi, you were lazy and treated my gift as if it were your right," Barbara shrugged, "I knew you weren't at home doing what I asked, I knew you hadn't locked the house, so I thought I'd hire a moving company and teach you a lesson."

"I'm lazy?" Jordi asked, "you think I'm the lazy one?"

"Jordan, please, you are giving me a headache."

"I thought you were dying. I thought you wouldn't make it past this fright- I cared for you- I looked after you-"

"You cared for me?" Barbara asked, "you barely did anyth-"

"I was in shock too. I was scared my grandmother was dying, I was scared my friend would never make it out of bed, I was scared we were going to be homeless without a way to put food on the table. And it was because of you that I was so scared."

"You have a funny way of showing you felt scared."

"Sorry that I didn't run around screaming and stealing furniture. Or faking my own illnesses so I could be waited on hand and foot. Did you know this plan for the home to go to Elizabeth has been in the works this whole time?"

"What do you mean? That Elizabeth has been planning this for a long time, I'm not surprised," Barbara said with her nose in the air.

"The whole family knew about it. They planned for you to live in a retirement home and they planned for me to be here for the short term."

"They planned this?"

"Good to know I wasn't the only one kept in the dark."

"They all planned this?" Barbara's eyes filled with tears, "they knew what was happening and did nothing? Typical."

"Worse," Jordi said, "they encouraged it. And honestly, it's about time you learned a lesson."

Jordi walked out the door, slamming it shut.

Chapter 21

Jordi ran down to the basement with Faith.

"She didn't know," Jordi said, puffing from the physical exercise.

"Yeah, weird," Faith acknowledged, "your family sounds like master manipulators."

"Can you believe no one told me?" Jordi said, slumping herself into the permanent dent on the left most cushion, "would you let your family member sit and stew in their own self doubt and guilt that was engineered by the people they believed loved them the most?"

"No Jordi," Faith said, "I wouldn't."

"Maybe I do need to move on from them."

"Move on, how?"

"Get a job, my own place, stand on my own two feet. Not have to rely on them," Jordi said, "I've always relied on my family and assumed they'd take care of me but I'm not so sure anymore."

"Family will always be there for each other but there's only so much people can give, you have to give back to your family too."

"Faith," Jordi said.

"Yeah?"

"I think you're my family."

"Of course I am, Jordi, don't be silly," Faith said, "I'm here for you through thick and thin and I know you're here for me too. Now, do you wanna play a game of pool?"

"You know what's weird," Jordi said, "I actually don't know if I'm happy to have my things back. I feel like I should be happy but I just don't connect with the stuff like I used to."

"That might be a good thing," Faith said, "you did spend an unhealthy amount of time down here."

"No I didn't," Jordi protested.

"Yes you did."

"No, I didn't."

"Yes. You did."

"You have a dent in the couch deep enough for Billy T. James to jump into," Faith said, grabbing a pool stick and setting up the balls.

"Well, I don't want to sit in it anymore," Jordi said, grabbing her a pool stick too.

"That's growth," Faith said, missing the white ball. She stood up straight, took a breath, took another shot and sank the eight ball immediately, losing the game.

"So. I won, Faith," Jordi said, "do you want to visit Michelle again?"

Jordi sat at Maggie's dining room table with a laptop in front of her while her friend snacked on cheese and crackers and chatted away to Maggie. Michelle was still fast asleep in her bed.

"She's been drinking Weetbix with milk and a bit of peanut butter. Sometimes I add frozen fruit but it makes the smoothie too thick for her to drink it," Maggie explained.

Jordi created a template for her CV.

"What should I put for 'work history'?" Jordi asked.

"Oh, you've done lots of things," Maggie said, "you've been a carer for, oh how long has it been?"

"About a year," Jordi said.

"There you go," Maggie said, "And you're so good with Michelle, say you've been a carer for two years, and put me down as a reference."

"Thanks, Maggie," Jordi said typing away at the laptop.

"Make sure you put caring down as one of your skills," Maggie said.

"Alright," Jordi agreed, typing away, "what are my other skills?"

They went silent and thought for a bit.

"Reliable," Faith said, "jobs love reliable people."

"Reliable. Done," Jordi said.

"Good people skills," Maggie said, "communication. That's an important skill."

"Done," Jordi said.

"You did manage to throw a fake party for Barbara in a short amount of time," Faith said, "that's a skill."

"How would I put that?" Jordi asked.

"Resourcefulness," Maggie said.

"I think this is brilliant," Jordi said, "oh my god- no it doesn't matter now."

"What?" Faith asked. They all looked at Jordi with suspicion and curiosity.

"Barbara told me her real birthday was this weekend," Jordi said, "but it doesn't matter now, we're both being kicked out."

"Jordan," Maggie said in shock, "just because things are not going well for you does not mean you can just forget those around you and I am shocked you would even suggest that, is that how you would treat Michelle?"

"No," Jordi hung her head.

"No," Maggie repeated, "I didn't think so. So do not treat Barbara that way, she is your grandmother and deserves your respect."

"I don't even know where to start," Jordi said, focusing back to the laptop, "all these office admin jobs either sound boring or require experience."

"Why are you going for an admin position?" Maggie asked.

"That's what I did for Barbara for a little bit," Jordi said, "that was the only job I've ever had."

"You've been a carer for Barbara and for Michelle," Maggie said, "look at carer roles, that's what we've been saying."

Jordi was silent for a moment, "they all want someone with a nursing degree."

"Really?" Maggie asked, "go back to those office admin jobs then."

"Even though they look boring? It seems all you do is go grocery shopping and clean," Jordi said looking through a job description.

"We all have to start somewhere," Maggie said, "click apply and see what happens."

Jordi clicked apply while Maggie and Faith chatted amongst themselves.

"I've applied to five," Jordi said.

"That's a great effort," Maggie encouraged, "but you had better get to Barbara's and buy her something nice for her birthday, here, take these."

Maggie pulled out Scorched Almonds from her cupboard.

"Where'd you get these?" Jordi asked.

"They came in a food box from the city mission but I think you need them more, go on."

Chapter 22

Jordi and Faith drove back to Barbara's. As soon as they parked the car Jordi's blood started to boil. "You okay?" Faith asked.

Jordi looked as though she was in a trance. She held the scorched almonds so tightly she poked a hole in the box.

"Barbara!" Jordi stormed into the house, "Barbara!" She walked right into Barbara's bedroom, where Barbara was sitting up on her bed with her fingers in her ears.

"Jordan, please," Barbara said, "my ears are far more delicate than yours."

"Are they?" Jordi asked. She threw the scorched almonds onto the bed in front of Barbara.

"Happy birthday," Jordi said as though she was in a torture chamber being forced to express love for her captors.

"I can't eat these, Jordan," Barbara said, "but thank you, I used to love these back in the day when my teeth were stronger. They bring back lovely memories."

"Good," Jordi said, "don't eat them."

"What is wrong with you?" Barbara said, looking taken aback, "that is not how you give a gift."

"You took my furniture," Jordi stated, "you took my things and you acted as though it had been you and only you that had been violated."

Barbara composed herself and spoke calmly back to Jordi, "In a way, it was me that was violated. In a way, it was me that had their business go up in flames. In a way, it was me who needed to be taken care of and was left with broken light bulbs, heavy curtains and chicken nuggets for dinner every night."

"Those chicken nuggets were chickenless and they were delicious," Jordi growled.

"They were not delicious," Barbara corrected, "And you are right, I took your furniture because I did not believe you had earned the right to sit on your bottom all day."

Jordi's lips thinned, "not everyone gets everything handed to them. Just because you were so lucky doesn't mean you get to judge others for their choices. Not everyone has a parent that will wait on them hand and foot and buy them whatever they want on a whim." Jordi's cheeks were fire.

"Are you saying that you are someone who does not have things handed to them?" Barbara asked, "are you saying you have had to work for a living and that everything you have, everything you own, and everything that aids in your lifestyle has been earned by you?"

"Yes," Jordi said, "as a matter of fact, I do have to work for everything that I have. I haven't had anything handed to me, in fact-"

"You have a great-aunt that is letting you live in her house, live in her basement that is set up for someone incredibly spoiled. I ask you to do work for me that never gets done. Never," Barbara said, "I let you eat my food, drive my car, and live under my roof all while getting yourself a weekly income for absolutely nothing, so yes, I thought you needed to learn a lesson."

Jordi looked at Barbara who sat on her bed so calmly and sternly. She held her ground and stared down Jordi who was looking at her with real, honest pain in her eyes. She felt a tightening in her gut and a stabbing in her heart as she realised she was looking at a reflection of herself.

Jordi stepped back and took note of what Barbara had said. This was a woman who had everything handed to her and had not learnt how her actions affected others. Exactly what Jordi was being accused of now. Jordi looked at the woman who could have done so much with her life, achieved so much, and helped so many people but instead she decided to indulge herself in television and manipulation to achieve what she felt was only fair. Exactly what Jordi was doing. Jordi looked at her reflection but didn't like what she saw. She left the bedroom and closed the door behind her, quietly.

Downstairs, Jordi sat on her old cushion with the old dent and the old anger stirring up inside her. She held her old controller as she looked at her old TV hanging back on the wall. She looked over at her pool table with all the pool cues laying on top of it. She no longer felt the comfort and the safety from this room she once required, these things no longer brought her into a fictional world where she felt she had more control. She no longer needed these escapes from reality, what she needed was a new reality and one that didn't rely so heavily on Barbara.

"You okay?" Faith asked from the corner of the room.

"She just said she saw me as someone who was a little bit, tiny bit, just a tad spoiled and felt it was in her right to take my things for no reason," Jordi said.

"That's horrible," Faith said, "Jordi, we don't have to stay here. We can leave right now and you can stay with my parents."

"No," Jordi shook her head and looked over at Faith.
"We can spend a few days playing pool and living our
best lives," Faith said, "It's always best to enjoy what
you have while you have it."
"What will you do when we have to move out?" Jordi
asked.
"What do you mean?" Faith asked, "I'm taking Billy T.
James and we're going home. I'm going to sleep in my
own bed and follow my routine like a sane person.
And I'm going tonight."
"You're taking Billy T. James?"
"Barbara asked me to take care of him."
"That's nice," Jordi smiled.
"What will you do, Jordi?"
Jordi shrugged and shook her head, "I guess I'll see
where the wind takes me, not a lot of choice so
hopefully I find a paying job soon."
"You've applied and that's a start," Faith said, "you
could follow up with an email if you were keen, it might
help you stand out from the crowd."
"Maybe."
"Wanna play Singstar? For old times sake."

Chapter 23

The basement stairs started to creak as Jordi's great-aunt, Barbara, came down the stairs. Barbara carefully placed each foot slowly on the next step and used the walls surrounding the stairs to balance herself. Barbara was 80 and needed support around the house. She struggled to walk up and down staircases but she braved this difficult venture when

she needed to talk to Jordan, as projecting her voice
caused her more trouble than walking down the stairs.
Barbara wobbled on the last step but regained her
balance just in time. She grabbed the doorknob at the
bottom of the stairs and with all her energy she turned
it with both hands and pushed through.

"Jordan," Barbara stood in the doorway watching the
women singing their hearts out. The two of them
laughed as Jordi sang out of key.

Jordi turned her head, noticing Barbara and her face
fell.

"What is it?" Jordi asked.

"You're not doing what you're supposed to," Barbara
smiled, "you're both so young," Barbara commented,
"you're both so beautiful."

"Thank you," Faith said with a note of confusion.

"You're so capable of so much," Barbara looked
longingly at the two.

"We are," Faith agreed.

"If I was your age again I'd be out there running
amuck," Barbara said, "showing the world what I was
made of. I wouldn't have the business again, no, that
ruined everything."

Barbara shook her head, "I don't think I would work at
all if I could live my life over again, I don't know what I
was thinking."

"Work is a good thing," Faith said, "we all need to do
it."

"No, not all of us," Barbara said, "Jordi and I don't
need to, we get everything handed to us."

"I'm going to start working for a living," Jordi said,
standing up and stretching.

"I've said that once, myself," Barbara said, "I used to pretend to work for a living but it was never enough, I always wanted more and was always given more. A bit like you, Jordi."

Faith glanced in Jordi's direction. Jordi's lips had thinned and her cheeks had grown red.

"But I must go," Barbara said, "do enjoy your game, I must pick my new accommodation for my apparent retirement. Good luck with your new accommodations."

Barbara hobbled back up the stairs, slow and steady. Every step she took creaked and she held her arms out against the walls to balance herself. The pain of giving up her home was sending her brain into a spin and the walls and the floor looked as though they were swapping places as she climbed higher. Barbara gave herself a moment to regain her proper eyesight, she sat down on the top step and placed her hand over her chest and felt the thumping of her heart beat. Her basement she so graciously had set up for Jordan had once been planned to be a teenage pad for her imaginary children. The kitchen was going to be where the chefs prepared meals for the family and the garden was perfect for gatherings with the grandchildren. There had even been a playground planned to be built once the first child came along, which never happened.

Barbara thought about the many wishes and wants she had believed would come true within this house. She thought about all the family gatherings she had planned but her parents and siblings had never made the journey across the water. She thought about the day Jordi's mother convinced her to take Jordi on as an employee, how forgetful and absent-minded she was. She thought about the conversations she had had where Jordi's mother grovelled and begged for Jordan to stay with her, learn from her and help her in her home. Those first few weeks were special, they almost felt as though Jordan was her very own. Jordan was keen to learn and ever so sorry for her past blunders; she tried to cook and clean and entertain Barbara with all the energy she could muster. Barbara remembered picking out the pool table for Jordan and her friends to enjoy, she thought it might even entice the wider family over to her home too. But nobody visited. She spoiled Jordan rotten thinking this would only show Jordan how appreciative she was to have the company in such goodwill. But one day Jordan became too comfortable. Jordan started to expect things to be handed to her. She expected chores to be done before she woke up in the morning. She expected for all of her wishes to be granted. Barbara understood how hard it was to be away from family and to have to make it on your own, so she allowed a bit of rest, and a bit more and a bit more until it felt like Jordan wasn't there to take care of her at all.

Barbara stood herself up off the stairway and made her way back up to her bedroom where she sat at her vanity that had been gifted by her father in his will. Barbara looked down at the brochures of Edmund Hillary Retirement Village her sister had sent her in the mail.

Barbara opened one and read all about assisted living. The photos showed people who were clearly far older than her, smiling and laughing. They all had grandchildren visiting and the little ones held pictures so proudly, showing their grandparent what they had drawn and coloured in. Barbara closed the pamphlet and put it facedown on the dark wood surface and covered it with a hat.

Chapter 24

The last two days in the house were spent with Jordi and Barbara avoiding each other. Barbara made her own meals and went out for short walks in her freshly trampled on garden, but she spent most of her time upstairs watching her TV.
Jordi spent all of her time in the basement with Faith. They played pool and reminisced about the life they once had here in Remuera.

"Do you remember that time we sang our karaoke so loud the neighbours made a noise complaint at two in the afternoon?" Faith asked.

Jordi giggled.

"I remember that time Barbara joined us for tea in the garden and we had to pretend like she had the most beautiful outdoor space in the world," Faith remembered, "It didn't look as terrible back then, actually."

"Don't be rude," Jordi scolded.

"I'm not being rude," Faith said, "It's not rude if it's true."

"Truth is subjective," Jordi stated.

"Did you get any replies back from the jobs you applied for?" Faith asked.

Jordi shook her head, "none."

"Still early days," Faith reassured.

There was a loud knocking on the basement door.

"Who is it?" Jordi called. There was no answer but the doorhandle began to turn. The door creaked open and Elizabeth's head became visible.

"Hello, there," Elizabeth said with a cheery, bright smile.

"Hello," Faith said.

"Enjoying my house?" Elizabeth asked.

Faith and Jordi just looked at her.

"Hand over is today," Elizabeth said.

"Today?" Jordi asked.

"Today," Elizabeth affirmed.

"I don't know how Barbara is going to react to this," Jordi said.

"Your grandmother is already outside," Elizabeth
stated, "I do want to say that I am sorry for the way
things have panned out."
"Come on," Jordi said, taking Faith's hand, "it's time to
go."

Chapter 25

Jordi visited Barbara in her new home in an apartment
complex inside Edmund Hillary Retirement Village.
The apartment was the size of Jordi's basement with
its own kitchen, dining, lounge, bathroom and a
separate bedroom. The bedroom even had a little
deck that looked down upon the courtyard and rose

garden with games like giant chess and outdoor bowls.

"Your place looks nice," Jordi commented, looking all around the room.

"Can you believe they tried to put me in hospital level care?" Barbara scoffed from her armchair facing the TV that was not turned on.

"What was it like?" Jordi asked.

"It was like a hospital but everyone was old," Barbara commented.

"Are you happy I'm here?" Jordi asked.

"Of course I am," Barbara said, looking up at her great-niece, "thank you for visiting."

"I thought the place would smell kind of weird but it doesn't," Jordi said.

"Oh, well, that is the strangest sort of compliment I have ever heard," Barbara said, "have you looked outside?"

Jordi slid the glass doors open and looked down at the roses, there seemed to be one in every colour. Four women were playing a game of outdoor bowls, placing pillows under their knees for support and rolling each ball with immense precision.

"Do you play bowls?" Jordi asked.

"No, I'm not really into bowls," Barbara explained, "but they have a bingo club here and I've convinced a couple of my girlfriends to start playing here with me, it's good fun."

"So you like it here?" Jordi asked.

"It's not the worst place in the world," Barbara looked at Jordi's soft, young skin, "I hope you've started using night cream."

Jordi raised her eyebrows at her great-aunt.

"If not," Barbara said, "I'll buy you some for Christmas. I have a fantastic collection but your supple skin needs something a bit more gentle I would guess."

"Thank you," Jordi said, without an ounce of gratitude.

"Have you got yourself a job, Jordan?" Barbara asked.

"A job?" Jordi asked back.

"Yes," Barbara said, "do you have one? How are you supporting yourself?"

"I haven't got myself a job yet," Jordi said, "the market's pretty thin."

"Of course it is," Barbara said, "all my friends' grandkids are moving to Australia, have you thought about doing that?"

"I've thought about it," Jordi said, "but it would cost a lot of money."

"And you would have to work a real job, too," Barbara said, "best not go to Australia, I think."

"I could go if I wanted to," Jordi said.

"Yes, yes," Barbara said, "we would all go if we wanted to."

Jordi looked around at Barbara's small apartment, "does this space work for you?"

"It's easier to get around which is nice," Barbara said, "And I have all my meals prepared for me, three times a day, and not once have I had to have chicken nuggets."

"But have you had chickenless chicken nuggets?" Jordi asked.

"I haven't had to have that either," Barbara said.

"That must suck," Jordi said, "I'm so sorry."

"I'm not."

Jordi smiled, "well, I'm glad things are working out for you here. I must be off and head onwards towards my responsibilities."

"You have responsibilities?" Barbara asked, "what on earth could they be."

"I help people in need," Jordi said.

"Good, it's about time," Barbara stated, "it's almost lunch so I had better make my way to the restaurant and see what it is they are serving."

"That sounds nice," Jordi said.

"Yes," Barbara nodded, "It turns out my sister is not so evil after all."

Chapter 26

"How's Billy T. James?" Jordi asked Faith, while patting him on her bed.

"He's really good," Faith said, "It was so nice of Barbara to let me take him but he's super needy."

"How so?"

"Look at him, he won't tolerate being alone," Faith said, "I guess he misses Barbara."

"Her apartment is nice," Jordi said, laying down next to Faith.

"I'm glad it's nice," Faith said, "does she seem happy?"

"She does," Jordi said.

"And you?" Faith asked, "how was your shift at Auckland City Mission?"

"It was hard. Life feels hard," Jordi said, "It's been difficult coming to terms with everything."

"Why don't we visit Michelle tomorrow and see how she's going?" Faith suggested.

"Maggie said she's been sitting up," Jordi said, "And holding conversation, so I think that would be nice."

The next day Jordi and Faith knocked on Maggie's door and received a squeeze of a hug.

"Jordi, come in," Maggie said, guiding her through the door.

"Thanks, Maggie. How's she doing?" Jordi asked.

"Come and see," Maggie opened the door to Michelle's room. They each stood on either side of Michelle's bed, looking at this person sitting up against pillows piled up vertically along the headboard.

"Michelle," Jordi rushed to wrap Michelle up in her arms.

"Hi Jordi," Michelle smiled at her. Michelle's bruise had completely healed and her face was back to a clear pale sickly colour.

"Don't wear her out with too much excitement," Maggie said, "I know that's old fashioned but I do have hopes that she'll be out of this bed before Christmas."

"She'll be out of it well before then," Jordi said, "how are you feeling?"

"Tired," Michelle answered, "but I can sit up in bed now and I'm back on solid food. Mum's a good cook but her smoothies are no match to mine."

"We thought about making your signature smoothie for you," Faith said.

"I think mum tried but no one makes it better than me," Michelle smiled a cheeky smile towards her mum.

"You're doing amazing," Faith said to Maggie, "look at how healthy you've gotten her."

Maggie smiled and nodded in appreciation.

"I'll make you all biscuits," Maggie said, running out towards the kitchen.

"I almost got myself a gig," Faith said.

"You've had lots of gigs," Michelle said.

"A real one," Faith said, "I auditioned to perform in the buskers festival this year."

"That's great," Michelle said, "I'm sure you'll get it next year."

"Thanks Michelle," Faith said with sarcasm.

"Faith was so close to getting it," Jordi said.

Michelle let out a weak giggle, "I bet she was."

"Jordi's been helping out at Auckland City Mission, building up a bit of work history," Faith bragged.

"Mum's been getting food boxes from there recently," Michelle said, "I think my illness has been making her really struggle."

"She seems like she's doing so well," Faith commented.

"She's a strong woman," Michelle said, "but we've been digging into savings and I think she's almost run out."

"I'm so sorry to hear that," Jordi said, her eyebrows knitting together.

"It is what it is," Michelle smiled, "we're doing our best. We're lucky we have a bit of support in this country."

Jordi nodded, "have you been getting Weetbix week on end?"

"Yes," Michelle giggled, "but it's good. Mum's been using it for my smoothies. The milk powder is something I've had to get used to though."

"Someone donated, like, a million boxes so now we have to get rid of them," Jordi said.

"Weetbix and milk powder, it's better than nothing," Faith said.

"Certainly better than nothing," Jordi agreed.

"No, I realise I'm really lucky," Michelle said, "not everyone gets the help we do."

"How much help are you actually getting?" Faith asked, "If you don't mind me asking."

"Mum and I are on a benefit, it probably equals to one decent full time income and then she gets a food box," Michelle said.

"What about medical?" Faith asked, "Is there anyone who can help look after you or help support your mum?"

"Not that I know of," Michelle said, "We're on our own in that regard."

Jordi slipped out of the room, trying not to interrupt their conversation.

"Maggie?" Jordi said, closing the door behind her.

"Hello, love," Maggie said, mixing the cookie dough.

"Can I talk to you?"

"Of course, what's wrong?" Maggie put the bowl down on the bench. She raced over to Jordi and guided her to the couch where they both sat, "you can talk to me about anything."

"I'm really struggling," Jordi said with a little lip wobble.

"Life can be really hard sometimes," Maggie said, placing a hand on Jordi's knee, "everyone needs someone to lean on. What can I do to help?"

Jordi looked at this woman who gave so much of herself to those around her and never once asked for anything back.

"I'm finding it really hard staying with Faith. I don't want to sound ungrateful and her family is lovely, I just don't get to have my own space over there."

"I'm so sorry, love," Maggie coo'ed, "can you take yourself off for walks? You can come and hang out here anytime, you know we have a spare room you can use as a quiet space."

"I think with all the changes that have been going on, I just need some place quiet to get a good sleep," Jordi explained, "did you know Faith snores?"

Maggie laughed, "I didn't know that."

"I'm just so lonely and even though Faith is doing a really nice thing, I just don't feel like she understands what I'm going through."

"What do you think you'll do?" Maggie asked with deep concern in her voice.

"I have no idea," Jordi said, "my mum has suggested I just stick it out. She reckons the best thing is to just push through but without a job, I'm just a burden on Faith's family."

"No!" Maggie exclaimed, covering her mouth with her hand, "you are not a burden, Jordi."

"I feel like one," Jordi said.

"Don't you ever say that," Maggie said, "just thinking you could think that breaks my heart."

"Do you think…" Jordi started, "do you think I could…"

"You have to stay here," Maggie said, "that's final."

"No, no, I couldn't," Jordi said with little resistance.

"You have to," Maggie urged, "we have a spare room and it will be so lovely to have another young one in the house."

"I'll help out of course," Jordi said, "I can cook dinners and keep the house clean and take care of Michelle, I've done it before, I wouldn't stay here for nothing."

"Jordi, you are more than welcome to stay here for nothing, it's our pleasure," Maggie said, patting her on the knee, "I'll make up the guest room now- oh but Jordi."

"Yes?" Jordi asked.

Maggie's cheeks went a light pink, "you should know I have had to give up my job recently to care for my little baby girl. She is so strong going through what she is going through-"

"She is," Jordi agreed.

"I've had to leave my job which means we are struggling a little bit in this house at the moment," Maggie explained, "the groceries are a little slim but we always make do."

"That's okay," Jordi said, "I can contribute with some of my government benefit and I'll get food boxes as well, which I can-"

"You'll do no such thing," Maggie said, "oh, Jordi, that's not right, not for you, you must move in here right away and I'll take care of you."

"Okay," Jordi nodded, "but not for nothing, we can set up a roster and take shifts for- uh- taking care of the place."

Maggie looked at Jordi with glassy eyes, "something about you feels very grown up now, Jordi."

Jordi smiled at Maggie.

"Go back and tell Michelle," Maggie said, going back to mix her biscuit dough.

Jordi slipped back into Michelle's room. Trying not to interrupt Faith and Michelle's conversation for a second time.

"Where have you been?" Michelle asked.

"How do you feel about me staying for a while?" Jordi asked.

www.ingramcontent.com/pod-product-compliance
Lightning Source LLC
Chambersburg PA
CBHW061323200626
46813CB00017B/2824